THE ENGLISH TUTOR

THE ENGLISH TUTOR

a novel by
JEFFREY ROUND

A broken promise. A forbidden love.
An act of redemption beyond imagining.

QUEERMOJO
A Rebel Satori Imprint
New Orleans & New York

Published in the United States of America by
REBEL SATORI PRESS
www.rebelsatoripress.com

ISBN: 978-1-60864-355-4

For those who struggle
For those who fail
For those who die

Touch has a memory. O say, love, say,
What can I do to kill it and be free …?
— John Keats

BURIAL

It's over. Everything culminates here in this pile of stones. Stepping back, I see what looks like a small statue or even a Buddhist shrine. But really, it's just a pile of stones. Not much to show for a hard night's labor on my part. It seems like just one more failure in a long line of failures visited on me over the last six months, rather than the end of an impossible quest. In any case, it's too late now for regrets.

I waited all day with growing impatience for the sun to set. At last, it slipped below the horizon as an immense darkness came over the city. I lingered in the café until I saw my face reflected in the windowpane and could be sure no one was watching. Then, without seeming haste, I paid my bill and hailed a cab. We were halfway to the palace grounds when I told the driver to stop and let me out on the side of the road. He shook his head, muttering something incomprehensible as I handed over my money and got out of the cab. I must have seemed like a crazy person. Little does he know.

I waited till his headlights disappeared around a curve and I found myself alone in the darkness. Still thinking about being followed, I glanced over my shoulder from time to time as I walked the rest of the way on foot. It took almost an hour to get here. I was tired even before I began digging, but I soon felt revitalized, almost exhilarated once I started.

Not surprisingly, the grounds were deserted apart from a few shadowy figures scavenging and flitting about inside the hulking remains of the abandoned buildings. He wasn't easy to find in the dark. Everything looks different by moonlight. My first thought was that someone had moved him, but I finally found him wedged between two slabs of concrete a little off the main path, right where I had left him. Even by daylight, you wouldn't be likely to have seen him unless you knew where to look. Not that anybody would be looking. To the world, he was gone and forgotten.

When I was sure no one was watching, I set about gathering the stones. That was the hardest part. I quickly realized I'd underestimated the difficulty of the task. There were plenty of bricks and chunks of broken concrete lying around, but that was not what I was after. The rocks were not as easy to dig up as I had anticipated.

I made a pile next to his body, keeping upwind to avoid the smell of decay. Once I'd gathered everything I could within reach, I headed farther out to forage for more. I carried the stones back one or two at a time, working through the evening and well into the night. For the most part, I had to dig with my bare hands and shoes, scraping my fingers and stubbing my toes more times than I can recall. The only reliable tool I had was a rusty piece of rebar. I hadn't brought anything with me to dig. It was better that way, though. A shovel and pickaxe would have made far too much noise, even out here in the middle of nowhere. I couldn't risk getting caught before I finished.

As I worked the moon rose full and bright, shining a clear

pathway across the sand. The darkness shrank around me and the sky filled with a false glow, as if dawn were not far off. Anyone watching would have wondered why I was shifting rocks in the middle of the night. Like the cab driver, they would have thought me a madman, or a prisoner doing penance. Then again, that's exactly what I am — a prisoner of a mad love doing penance for my crime.

Whenever anyone approached I hid myself in the rocks, waiting till the footsteps faded and whoever it was passed by. No one stopped to look or talk; for that I was grateful.

Once I'd collected the rocks, I gently began to cover him, first with the larger stones, then the smaller ones, finally filling the cracks with sand. Even that took longer than I expected.

I've always said that religion and politics lead to war: the fruit of both is death. I'm not the first to say it; others have said it far better than I have. I told him that right from the beginning, but he wouldn't listen. Now he is buried and his body hidden from sight, as I too am hidden from his eyes — those infinitely gentle, infinitely perceptive eyes that silently accused me of so many things when he was alive. But he understood something I didn't: that love, too, can kill. He always said I would kill him — I, who had only his best interests at heart. Only now do I see he was right.

BARS

It's difficult to pinpoint the beginning of our story, to say there was one particular moment in time that it sprang from, like Proust's *madeleine* dipped in a *tisane* of lime blossoms as a lifetime of visions arose magically from the steam. But if it is possible to choose just one moment then I'd say it was the Thursday before we actually met, like a seed planted unseen beneath the soil from which it will inevitably spring.

I hadn't planned on going out that night. In fact, I was determined to stay inside and read a book I had recently purchased, but some inner stirring said, No, let's have one more kick at the can. You're not so old you should spend all your evenings alone. There will be plenty of time for sitting around between endless rounds of Broadway singalongs and drag bingo after they stick you in the LGBTQ retirement home, if there is such a thing. It might even have been something to look forward to, if I were so inclined. I wasn't.

So then, if I were to choose just one out of the ten thousand possible moments that led me here, it would be that one. If you're inclined to be philosophical about these things, you might also say my location was to blame. When you live in a high-rise building with a striking view of the horizon, where you can watch the sky turn from blue to indigo to black each night, it's as if everything is tempting you to leave your solitude for the false promise of the city's lights. Without doubt that is what prompted me to put down the snore of a book I'd begun reading, don my jacket, and head out that particular evening. On the other hand, I could blame the author of that novel. If he'd written a more engaging story, then none of this might have happened. But, as I said, it's a bit late for regrets.

In fact, I was eager to experience a bit of fun. I'd been feeling bored and out of touch with life since my return from an extended stint in Europe — several years extended, in fact — which my mother referred to as my "second adolescence." It was what others might have described as "finding yourself," a euphemistic phrase that is in itself problematic if you think about it, begging as it does the question of why you would look for yourself in places you've never been before. For that I have no answer, except to say that I never found whatever part of me was missing. Or perhaps the part of me that was missing was really him. In which case, I would have to say I did find it after all. Only not where I expected.

"You've got a Doctorate in Philosophy, for god's sakes," my mother unhelpfully reminded me when I first announced my intentions of spending a year in Europe following my graduation. "It's time to get a job."

"Meaning I should engage in real life?" I suggested ironically, while imagining myself sipping a *Negroni* in some charming cafe in Rome.

"Yes, Geoffrey. You must take your future seriously. You need to be realistic,"

She sat there staring at me in her tailored Chanel outfit,

having just returned from her manicurist or pedicurist, or perhaps it was her hair stylist that day. Her upper-class accent, still hanging on more than two decades after leaving England, was especially pronounced at times like these. Nothing she said would have convinced me, however. I had closed my ears to her words, unwilling to let her dissuade me from what I'd already begun to think of as the most glamorous period of my life, a time of unparalleled freedom from duties and responsibilities.

"Get your feet on the ground, Geoffrey. You need to start a family." These were her final words, uttered on her way out of a room whose temperature had dipped precipitately since the onset of our discussion.

Her suggestion that I get a job sounded not unwise, just unwanted. I preferred the prospects of imbibing culture and pursuing a life of the mind over the prospects of foraging for a living. I'd already cast myself in the role of aesthete, not day laborer. As well, her latter suggestion — that of starting a family — was yet another dig at the probability, as she saw it, that I would sow my seed on barren soil for the rest of my days. The topic of my sexuality provided ample ammunition to avenge herself for all sorts of slights, both real and imagined, committed by me. She seldom missed an opportunity to take aim and let go another salvo. Why live in peace when the possibility of conflict lay all around you? That seemed to be my mother's credo.

In truth, my desire to leave home arose from a deeper, darker place: the need to free myself from the constraints of family life and the emotional blunting foisted on us by those who purport to love us best. Hidden anger and a barely submerged self-loathing have long been the hallmarks of my clan. Had we been medieval royals, there would have been a ritual blood-letting before each ascension to the throne as titles passed from fathers to sons, though I daresay the women wield the sharpest daggers behind the scenes. My family history is a cautionary tale in a book from which few have escaped alive to tell what lies between its pages.

In spite of my mother's reluctance to accept my decision to travel abroad — or perhaps because of it — I steadfastly refused to see the wisdom in her point of view. I already had a small inheritance from my father, then just recently deceased, and so had no need of her approval. As for getting my feet on the ground and obtaining something that amounted to work, the possibilities were few. With my come-hither looks and smooth manners, I might have wrangled a job at some over-priced perfume counter in chichi Yorkville, enticing lonely, neglected women to purchase things they didn't need, but then I was allergic to scents. Something to do with figures? Not a chance. I hadn't the head for them. My mind was perpetually in the clouds, as they say. And I loathed physical activity. I preferred art to business, reading to laboring. I was, however, good at argument and might have made a decent lawyer, but that would have entailed another four years at school. What did the world need with yet another lawyer?

So, practically speaking, during my "lost" years in Europe I made my way from one country to another by teaching English to bored, wayward children of the middle classes, from backgrounds as pampered as my own. These were children who had no interest in learning, I might add, and whose parents' real intentions lay in having an exotic babysitter for their progeny more than anything educational. As it turned out, however, I was good at it, and the hours it entailed did not disrupt my true aim of living a life of culture and leisure in some of the world's most beautiful cities. So I put up with them as the first year extended to another and yet another. Then, suddenly, it was over. My inheritance had dwindled precipitously. The European Union, likewise, showed signs of becoming unsettled if not altogether unraveled, and I discovered that the work no longer sustained me. So I reluctantly returned to a city I had not lived in for the better part of a decade, while resolving not to ask my mother for assistance, financial or otherwise.

I returned home to live with a friend. Or rather, to stay in the apartment of a friend while he was away on an acting gig. Jerod and I often provided for one another, loaning out residences abroad if one or the other of us happened to be in need. I have a particular bent for Paris, which Jerod also loves, so he always managed, despite being a poor thespian, to scrape together the money for a visit. I, on the other hand, often had an apartment in Paris, but never quite enough funds to live on, so Jerod and his spare change were welcome whenever he felt the need for a visit.

"*Paris, c'est moi!*" Jerod would cry, despite the fact that he was a black, non-French-speaking actor.

In the end I would have done just about anything to prolong my stay in Europe, preferring to smoke and drink and chat on the balcony of some cheap, bedbug-ridden hotel overlooking the Seine rather than return to the lap of my mother's world of sterile luxuries. But, as I said, my money ran out and I could see no alternative to returning home to face the so-called realities of the working world.

Impractical as I may paint myself to be, I came back fully intending to face my demons. I had for so long evaded them by lingering in a post-graduate haze of waiting for one's life to begin, that I was able to convince myself it might be a novelty to get a job. If I'd known then what else it would bring, I might have tried harder to stay away.

"Now that you're back, what are you going to do?" my mother asked on my return, looking both pleased and smug at the same time, as only she could manage with her surgically limited range of facial expressions.

"Yes, that's the question, isn't it?" I replied evasively, still not of the mindset that one must always *do* something to justify one's existence. Why wasn't *being* ever enough? It was good enough for Aristotle. If only those spiritually bankrupt Europeans hadn't come along and muddied the waters with their questions about being and nothingness all those centuries later, we might all have been left in peace.

There are two Chinese expressions that may shed light on my world view. The first is purportedly a curse: *May you live in interesting times*. While the better part of my life has been anything but predictable, it has always been interesting. The second seems more indicative of my life as it has unfolded over the past half year: *He who rides the tiger can never get off*. While frequently insightful, I note that Chinese proverbs are not often jolly. I have now dismounted my tiger and await the consequences.

In any event, the night I met my tiger — or rather the night

I almost met him, as it turned out — I was living downtown when the urge I'd been resisting all evening took a decisive turn. I put down the extremely dull book being hailed as that season's sensation, donned a light jacket and stepped out. There I found myself on the strip yet again, a jaded, slightly over-the-hill rebel looking for his cause.

For those of us who grew up in the disheveled ash-heap of history known as the second half of the twentieth century, change was a constant. It was as though we were all in some intangible way searching for a place to belong as much as we were looking for a sense of identity. May you live in interesting times indeed.

As I made my way to the gay neighborhood on the evening in question, I noted with irony that, in attempting to escape the dreary prison of our lives, so many of us turn to temporary habitations called "bars." In our twenties, we see them as magical places to meet new friends and have any number of adventures. By our thirties, however, and especially if you've been around as much as I have, they no longer have such an appeal. Sad to say, if you haven't developed a proper social life by then you probably never will. Still, companionship, even of a limited sort, is a welcome diversion. I don't particularly enjoy socializing in public spaces: I particularly dislike piano bars with their sad, sing-a-long sentiments, and I no longer have the urge to gyrate and spin the night away in the disco palaces of my wasted youth. But the truth is, I just don't like spending the evening alone.

Part of the problem with living abroad is that the allure of being out on the town takes on a greater sheen of urgency. It's easy to convince yourself that you're in a hub of culture and that people just like you — fun, congenial people with interesting lives, or so we would like to think — are winging their way from all over the globe to gather in this nexus where you might just conceivably meet the man of your dreams. There's always the hope that your fate is heading towards you and that one day, in the right time and place, you will recognize it. Odd then that I met mine not in Paris or London or Istanbul, but much closer to home.

On that particular night, I found myself on the patio of a bar largely frequented by older men. Perhaps it was a matter of keeping both the competition and lighting to a minimum, so I would always appear to have the age advantage. Or maybe, as I tell myself, it's simply that older men have more interesting things to say. I remained optimistic in that regard as I made my way upstairs to the patio.

I should explain that some people think me a snob. I prefer to think that I am just particular about the company I keep. Even beggars should be choosers, I feel. I often make friends with bartenders for that reason. Whenever a bore looks as though he might try his chances with me, I simply start up a conversation with someone guaranteed to stay on the right side of things. But patios are a lawless sort of territory, a sexual wild west where anything goes.

I had scarcely been there a minute when I was approached by an attractive man perhaps a decade older than me. His hair gleamed silver, as though to guarantee that he qualified for the category of silver daddy then very much in vogue.

"Hi, I'm Bob," he said without hesitation.

"Geoffrey."

Without asking, he sat beside me. Catching a whiff of an accent, I ventured an inquiry.

"South Africa," he replied with an enigmatic smile.

It was not a country I was familiar with. I plied him with the usual questions: what was it like? Why had he come to this country? Would he stay long?

"Why so curious?" he asked, when I persisted with my questions.

Obviously I'd put him off, but he had invited himself to sit with me. The least he could do was prove interesting. I replied that I'd never been to South Africa. Having heard conflicting things, it made me wonder.

"It's not an easy place to live at the moment," he said, as though explaining a complex political perspective to a relative simpleton. "In any case, conversation isn't what I'm here for."

He placed a hand on my knee, giving it a vigorous rub. I was disappointed to find that intellectual companionship wasn't his real interest.

"And that's not what I'm here for," I replied.

He gave me a cynical smile.

"It's what we're all here for, sweetheart."

"Then I've been misinformed." I shrugged and held up my beer. "Besides, it's early. This is only my first."

He stood.

"I'll come back and check again in a while," he said. "Maybe the alcohol will loosen you up."

Don't count on it, I wanted to reply as he headed off to the darkened maze at the far end of the bar. Perhaps there he'd meet his match, since an intellectual pairing wasn't in the cards for him that night.

I leaned against a wall and downed my beer, wondering whether to have a second. What I lacked at that moment, besides companionship, was a cigarette. I wasn't about to make the mistake of asking for one from any of the men in my vicinity, however, as it might give the wrong impression. I was lonely, yes, but I had come there mostly to observe. To observe what, I couldn't say. If nothing else, there was the unsullied purity of the night sky peeking out from above the surrounding high rises.

I leaned, I lacked, and I swigged from my nearly empty bottle of beer. I didn't look at the men around me who might attempt to catch my attention, however, but at the ones already engaged in conversation. As an observer of human behavior, I prefer it in its purest form: when the observed does not know he's being watched.

Giant television screens had been positioned so that no matter where you turned you were confronted by images of men coupling — pornography, I mean — as though to suggest possible permutations of what awaited the bar's clientele if they played their cards right with various South Africans and whatnot. I shifted and twisted, but there was no angle from which I could avoid the soft glow of the screens. Maybe Bob was right: it was what everyone went there for.

It was at that moment I realized I had turned from watcher to watched, from observer to observed. Against a far wall, a young man in a leather jacket seemed to be mimicking my pose. I saw a mysterious smile and a mane of long, curly hair

[13]

peeking out from under a grey hoodie. In the dim light, his features appeared Gallic. He sported a wild, bohemian dress.

I shifted my pose; he shifted his to match. He continued to stare with a peculiar intensity. At least I must have some sex appeal left, I noted wryly. Not that it did much good if all I could attract were counter-culture types. After a minute, I tired of the game and went back inside. There I found a different wall to lean against, this one out of range of the galvanizing videos with their mesmeric promises.

Here I focused on the men lined up at the bar. Before long, however, I felt a creeping sensation running up the back of my neck. I turned. There he was again, my own private stalker. In the light, he looked more Italian than French, as he stood against a far wall, once again mimicking my pose and observing me as I had done others. I noted with irony that I did not enjoy the feeling.

For a moment, I weakened. I thought I would acknowledge him, but then again — no. He wasn't my type. I wasn't into grunge rockers. My gut instinct also said he looked like far too much work for a one-night stand.

I glanced at the screens to my left and right. Overhead, and entirely out of reach, a trio of attractive young men were putting the make on one another. My prospects looked far less exciting than theirs. I set down my empty bottle, thankful yet again for having escaped the prison of the senses. Once again, Fate had not intervened. Mr. Right had not yet arrived. Or so it seemed to me at the time.

YUSUF

According to the Quran, Yusuf was a sixteenth-century BCE leader with the gift of prophecy. The eleventh son of the Israelite patriarch Jacob, his name means, "God increases in piety, power and influence." My Yusuf did not at first strike me as being a man of faith, though for all intents and purposes religion was inextricably intertwined with his nature. But let's leave him here for a moment, as I left him leaning against a wall in the bar when I first spotted him. I'll return to him at length, however, as this story concerns Yusuf above all.

I hadn't had much luck securing a job on my return. A trial ad on *kijiji* resulted in a few temporary work offers, but nothing more. So, too, with the notice I placed in some of the newspapers. It seemed the tide had turned, but not in my favor. I continued swimming upstream, struggling but slowly losing hope. Brave New World indeed. In Europe I had thrived on personal recommendations over the past few years. Now it seemed I needed to change my tactics if I wanted even just to survive.

It was a casual acquaintance who recommended offering my linguistic services to adults rather than children, suggesting I visit the various hospitals around the city. People with time on their hands might be more receptive to tutoring, he said.

Thinking it over, I decided I had nothing to lose. Famous last words.

The truth was, I missed working. I craved getting up in the morning with purpose and seeing all those bright, energetic young people to-ing and fro-ing between home and work each day, performing jobs that consumed their time and gave them just enough money to live on while getting them out into the world, where the whirl and bustle could shape them in ways they never dreamed of. All these years later I realized my mother was right: I'd spurned my chance to lead a normal life; now it was proving too late.

Undaunted, I got up early one morning armed with a handful of flyers, intending to post them at downtown hospitals. That was how I discovered a notice placed prominently on a community billboard asking for translators and English tutors for patients undergoing biomedical reconstructive surgery. It seemed to be a good sign.

A brief phone interview ensued. After I detailed my teaching history, there were a few questions.

"Are you a patient person?" I was asked.

Compared to what? I was tempted to ask. After all, I'd taught privileged children. You need patience to deal with pampered kids.

"I teach children," I said hesitantly.

"Yes — very good. Some of these men are like children," the voice informed me. "Are you experienced in dealing with people from other cultures?"

"Decidedly," I replied with greater confidence, though all I really wanted to know was what the job paid. "I taught English in six countries in Europe, five of them non-English-speaking countries."

The questions continued: "Have you worked with trauma victims before?"

"No," I answered truthfully, though I could have mentioned having had a great deal of experience at being traumatized by my family during my formative years.

"What about people who are on heavy medication for anxiety and stress?"

Again, I replied in the negative, thinking the job was sounding drearier and drearier at every turn. What was I letting myself in for? Surely something as involved as what my interviewer seemed to be describing required more than a glib facility for languages, perhaps something along the lines of a degree in psychotherapy.

I listened with diminished interest as the voice suggested I could be useful to the government by offering my services to a group of Libyans living in the city and receiving medical treatment for injuries sustained in combat. Even in Europe I had been only vaguely aware of the civil war raging in that country following an uprising against the dictator Muammar Gaddafi the previous year. These men, known as Freedom Fighters, were part of a larger Middle East revolt dubbed the Arab Spring, a rebellion being fought largely by ordinary citizens, workers and students.

As it was explained, they were not refugees but rather participants in a program sponsored by their country's post-revolution government, allowing them to partake of advanced medical treatment in other countries, my own included. The phone call concluded with my agreeing to an interview the following morning.

I had no great expectations, but I also had no other offers to consider. I decided to make an effort to appear as acceptable as possible to the program's coordinators as well as to the men who might be placed under my tutelage. If they liked me and wanted me, then I would decide.

I went home and dug through my closet for a suit from my student days, only to find I had outgrown them all. My mother watched curiously as I went through my father's closets next. I was surprised to see she had kept all of his clothing, which now fit me.

"I couldn't bear to give them up," she said sadly, shaking her head, as I wondered about this urge to cling to the dead.

I took a cab to the hospital the next morning, nervously straightening my tie and brushing a bit of dirt off my brown brogues right before I was ushered into a small waiting room. Various government representatives, both Libyan and domestic, greeted me and assured me they were glad of my offer to help. I was given a contract to read and sign in the event that I should be chosen to tutor the men selected for the program.

I was having concerns over my sexuality in light of the situation. While I'd known a few gay Muslims, I had never before worked with non-gay Muslims and was not looking forward to dealing with cultural prejudices. Then again, work was work and money was money. My sexuality would in no way prevent me from being an effective tutor.

It turned out there were five of us applying for the position, all of us men. Three were clearly straight, if my gaydar was to be trusted, while a fourth was ambiguous in his sexuality. I had the impression that thin, nervous Marcus, the project coordinator, was gay too, but if so he hid it well.

After a quick briefing that involved a few short speeches by various officials, the doors were reopened and we were led into another room where a group of fifteen dispirited-looking men waited. Some were in wheelchairs, while others had crutches at their sides. Most wore the beards and facial hair emblematic of adherents of Islam. The youngest, a boy of about twenty, caught my attention. He had a beautiful face and brooding, doleful eyes. His name was Hassan, I later learned. His left leg was missing below the knee.

I waited silently as we were introduced to the men and informed we would be available to them as English instructors. Some regarded us with open curiosity, while others reminded me of the bored-looking children forced to study by their over-zealous parents, whom I had tutored throughout Europe. It was only later that I learned to recognize the apparent lack of interest on these men's faces as a consequence of the heavy medication they were forced to take.

As I scanned the room, I glimpsed a face I recognized from somewhere. At first I couldn't place him. He stood in a corner away from the others, watching me, the only one whose features bore anything like a smile. I shifted my stance and he shifted his to match. I realized with a start that this was the long-haired young man who had followed me around the bar the previous week. Not Italian or French then, but an Arab. In a gay bar. And not just any Arab, either, but a Freedom Fighter. He certainly hadn't wasted time acclimatizing himself to our ways.

My eyes quickly searched his body for visible signs of injury. Where the others showed obvious trauma, with him I found none. I noticed, however, that he favored his left hand, keeping it tucked in the pocket of the same grey hoodie he'd worn in the bar when I first caught sight of him.

He seemed to pay no particular attention to me or the other tutors. Instead, he focused on the figure at his side, a large man with unkempt hair and a stony gaze, seated in a wheelchair and missing both legs above the knee. Although I couldn't know it, this man was already then, and would continue to be in future, an influential and divisive figure in the small group I was to tutor.

Right before the meeting ended, I stole another glance at the young man from the bar. He returned my gaze briefly then looked away. But it was enough for me to see in those eyes a kind of acknowledgement. That was as much as I would get from him that afternoon, however, with no further glimpse of what was to come before he changed my life forever.

COURSES

I felt a sense of relief mingled with curiosity on learning that I was one of three tutors chosen to instruct the Libyan Freedom Fighters. For the next few months, from Monday through Friday, I would teach five men in both individual and group settings. Classes were not held at the hospital, where the interview had taken place, but rather in a downtown hotel where many of the men were housed.

The following week I met with Marcus, the project's coordinator. We spoke at length about the expectations of both teacher and pupils. He stressed that the men were there for a limited time and their priority was reconstructive surgery, which often disrupted their daily schedules. After that, following a period of recuperation, they would be sent home. Whatever English they learned in the meantime was looked on by those in charge of the program as an additional benefit, but no more than that. I also sensed from what Marcus told me, though I never had it confirmed, that it was a means of keeping the men occupied during their recovery, distracting them from the psychological hardships they faced as war veterans and amputees, while steering them away from whatever potential difficulties they might encounter as they adjusted to life in the West.

I assured Marcus that I understood the aims of the program and would do my utmost to provide quality instruction to my students without burdening them with unreasonable demands and expectations. I was, once again, a nanny to a select group, though these were not the spoiled and pampered children of the well-to-do.

He thanked me and assured me he had faith in my ability to provide them with whatever help they required. Again, I felt that curious tingling that said he and I were cut from the same cloth.

We were soon joined by two of the men, whom Marcus introduced as Abdel and Hassan. Abdel was the large, gruff-looking double-amputee I had noted earlier. Even seated in a wheelchair, his presence was imposing. Hassan was the younger man with the looks of a matinee idol. He would no doubt have had access to a wheelchair, but had chosen to come to the class on crutches. This may have been a means of asserting his independence, though perhaps it was simply a test of his mobility. Both sported full beards, as was the Muslim custom. Apart from a curt greeting, neither of them spoke much, either to Marcus and me, or to each other, apart from an occasional comment in Arabic. Two others, Hamid and Ibrahim, soon joined us. It was by then already ten minutes past the appointed hour. Marcus glanced at his watch then turned to me.

"I think we can start. That's nearly everyone," he said. Then, in a quieter voice, he added, "You may occasionally have to retrieve them from their rooms if they don't show up. The drugs keep them in a perpetual haze and they often lose track of time. I'll make sure you have everyone's contact information before I leave."

He had just turned to the gathering when the door opened to admit a final student. It was the long-haired man I had seen at the bar the previous week. I caught the outline of muscular biceps and a well-developed torso. His facial hair was limited to a bit of scruff on his chin. He looked distinctly Western compared to the others. Looks of recognition passed between himself and the other men as he crossed the room with a long, lazy stride. On seeing him, I felt a moment of alarm, wondering if our worlds would collide in the coming sessions.

I put these thoughts aside as Marcus introduced him: Yusuf. The latecomer acknowledged me with a brusque nod then sat and focused on Marcus. Once again, I noted he kept his left hand tucked inside his jacket pocket.

After a brief introduction from Marcus, I stood and looked over the faces watching me. I wondered briefly how they saw me, their non-Muslim English teacher. Their expressions ranged from blank and glazed-over to downright curious. This was the moment I sized up my prospects, intuiting their levels of interest and probable success rate in the weeks and months ahead, as well as my future prospects in terms of further employment. For the first time in years I found it impossible to say exactly what I was facing, but I knew without doubt that in the coming days these men would challenge and test the limits of my capabilities.

"My name is Geoff Manderson. I am very happy to be your teacher," I said.

And with that simple statement, the class began.

My first course of action is always to establish the level

of competency in English each student has already attained. To my surprise, Abdel showed the greatest facility, both in grammar and pronunciation. Clearly, he'd studied the language. He confirmed this, saying he had taken two years of conversational English in high school. I commended his command of the language and asked him to tell us something about his personal life.

He explained that before the war he had been what sounded like a "mushroom farmer." Thinking I had misunderstood, I asked him to repeat himself. In fact, I had heard correctly the first time.

"Yes, I am a mushroom farmer," he said with a short laugh then nodded and turned things back over to me.

Hassan was a near beginner, though he'd picked up a few basic words since his arrival. He was shy, but seemed eager to learn. In my experience this type often proved the best student in the long run, so long as I could keep their interest and make them feel secure.

I turned to the others. Hamid, also in a wheelchair, was a scrappy type, bulky and energetic. He'd lost his right leg below the knee. Ibrahim, conservative in a suit and tie, was slightly older than the others. He was missing his left forearm. Both men had minimal fluency and, I sensed, minimal interest in whatever I could offer them, whether from a lack of interest in learning English or a lack of faith in me.

I turned to my final student, Yusuf.

"How do you like Toronto?"

"Yes, I like Toronto very much."

"Good." I nodded. "Have you ever been on the subway?"

"Yes."

"Can you elaborate?"

His confusion showed. "What is 'elaborate'?"

"It means, tell me more. When were you on the subway?"

"I am coming in Canada from Turkish on subway."

"You came to Canada from Turkey?" I asked.

"Yes. I am coming on subway for thirteen hours."

His right hand indicated something moving through the air.

"That was probably an airplane," I offered gently, not to make him feel belittled.

"This airplane?" he asked, making the same hand motion.

"Yes. I think it was an airplane that brought you here, not a subway."

His laugh was quicksilver, with no sign of embarrassment. "I like airplane!"

"Good, Yusuf. Do you recall which airline it was?"

His face furrowed for a moment then he said, "Crack."

Having got used to deciphering the seemingly unintelligible gibberish of my students for the past decade, I ventured an educated guess. "Do you mean Krakow Air?"

He broke into a broad smile. "Yes, from Polish!" he exclaimed enthusiastically. It was the tone he reserved for anything that pleased him, as I soon came to learn, and which I can still hear to this day.

Marcus fixed me with a look of amazement. Not only could I reach these men, he saw, but I seemed able to gaze into their psyches and grasp what was hidden at who knew what mysterious depths. I had just scored big points with the project coordinator. With any luck, I wouldn't be worrying about work in the foreseeable future, at least for as long as the project held out.

By the time the session came to an end an hour later, I had a good grasp of each man's capabilities. Marcus and I stood. Abdel and Hamid remained seated in their wheelchairs. Yusuf and the others slowly got to their feet. I shook hands with each of them in turn and was surprised by the warmth in their smiles. When I got to Yusuf, he held my gaze with his startling brown eyes.

"You are good teacher," he said with enthusiasm.

I thanked him, saying I was pleased to be his English instructor and that I looked forward to our next session together.

It was then that I glimpsed his left hand, or rather what remained of it: only the thumb was intact alongside the stumps of his fingers, each amputated below the first set of knuckles. It struck me then that I was whole and complete, while each of these men had suffered the loss of some significant part of their bodies. No amount of surgery was ever going to change that. Learning English was certainly not going to be a priority for them.

Marcus waited till all five of the men left the room and were headed down the hallway before turning to me.

"You've very quickly gained their confidence," he said. "It was clear they liked you."

"I'm glad," I said. "That helps a great deal in the learning, I find."

"Yes, clearly. This is significant in terms of what you can accomplish."

He handed me a sheet of paper with each of the men's

names and room numbers, as well as contact information for the project coordinators, including his own. I glanced over it quickly, hoping my face showed no great curiosity. Yusuf's, I saw, was the last name on the list.

"I'm very happy to entrust them into your hands," Marcus continued. "I'm sure you'll do an excellent job, but don't expect miracles. As I've said, their medication is taxing on both mind and body. Always be patient with them."

"I will," I assured him.

"You and I will keep in touch on a regular basis. I'll report back to the committee on the progress you make overall, but apart from an occasional drop-in I won't be attending the individual sessions. Any last questions?"

I didn't want to mention my concerns about my sexuality outright, but thought to ask obliquely.

"What about cultural differences? Is there anything I need to be aware of? Religious prohibitions, that sort of thing?"

He looked away for a moment. When he turned back, his eyes carried a knowing gleam.

"There are dietary restrictions, of course, but unless you're eating with them that needn't concern you. You might want to familiarize yourself with their religious customs, but it's not strictly necessary." He paused. "We don't judge other people's beliefs, even if we don't agree with certain cultural biases or outlooks."

Without stating it, Marcus had just told me that he was gay, or at least that he knew I was. He had also warned me to steer clear of trouble in that regard.

"I get you," I told him.

He blushed. Perhaps he realized he had given himself away. Maybe he even wanted a confidante of sorts.

"Don't be afraid to get to know them," he told me. "They're just men, like us."

In that, he couldn't have been more right.

MOTHER

I was of two minds with respect to telling my mother about the job. If she disapproved of it, she might make some slighting comment about my "wasted potential" and ruin my day. I resolved not to let her. While I was fairly certain she would approve of the charitable aspects of helping wounded soldiers, I doubted she would look kindly on that fact if she knew that they were rebel fighters from another country. The phrase "charity begins at home" takes on a very literal meaning in her mind.

As it turned out, I needn't have worried.

"I'm so happy to hear this!" she cried, as though I'd just announced my promotion to the position of CEO of some mega-corporation. "Tutoring English in a hospital. Wonderful!"

Somehow, her over-the-top reaction left me feeling more unsettled than if she'd been displeased or just lukewarm in her response. It was as if she were practicing reverse psychology in hopes of discouraging me from following through with my plans.

"It's just contract work" I told her, not to get her hopes up, and stemming further effusiveness on her part. "It will last as long as the project lasts and then I'll move on to other things."

She shook her head. "This will lead to better things once

they find out how good you are, Geoffrey. It's tremendous news! It will help you get your life back on track."

My mother has always been one for platitudes. They seem to bolster her belief that life need not ever get off track if one simply followed the rules as they are set forth. When I was growing up, she would recite these hackneyed phrases. "Respect your elders" was one she quoted often. For my part, I couldn't muster respect for people simply because they were older than me when proof of the mess they had made of the world was very much in evidence to my generation. And then there was that old chestnut, "Know your place," meaning not only as compared to your supposed betters, but also as regards those who might be below one's station in life. The latter must have seemed particularly apt in my situation, as I had spent much of my youth ignoring my privileged origins, in defiance of my mother's wishes that I might one day accept my true place in the world. To that end, she conducted her own genealogical research and discovered that the Manderson family name meant "Mindful of my origin," a phrase she repeated often and with great depth of feeling, as though in her eyes it was proof of some fundamental principle.

One must know one's station and not consort with the wrong types, she seemed to imply, perhaps feeling she herself had slid too far down the social ladder by marrying my father. In any case, she was more than capable of offering me shopworn platitudes, if not motherly love. No doubt she had higher expectations of the filial duty they would inspire in me in return.

Her other implication — that I had let my life get off track

— seemed less insulting than it might have had she made the comment on a day when my news was not as good as it was. I wasn't even sure I disagreed with her in principle.

"You must be very pleased," she continued.

"It does feel like a step in the right direction," I allowed, returning her comment with a platitude of my own.

"We'll celebrate. Let's go out for lunch. Where would you like to go?"

Knowing not to take my mother's momentary surge of generosity for granted, I quickly accepted.

Mangia e Bevi is one of the few "ethnic" restaurants whose food does not disagree with my mother's digestion. We were given a table on our arrival. She was effusive, charming the waiters and ordering with a flair that made it clear she was in charge and expected the very best of everything. At moments like these, I found her amusing rather than offensive, her British-ness shining through with its hints of snobbery like glints of semi-precious stones extruding from a slab of basalt.

She beamed at me over a glass of chardonnay that had been cut with soda. "Your father would be pleased to know that you're back home and following a positive course of action after all that time in Europe."

She looked away for a moment, as though the memory of my father had unsettled her. A typical corporate executive, he'd also been a chronic philanderer, straying repeatedly from my mother's charms. But then I wasn't sure if I blamed him, my mother's charm-offensive advisory often suggested donning the emotional equivalent of bullet-proof vests.

In her twenties, while still living in England, my mother had been a successful fashion model. It was just as she was outgrowing her prospects in that arena, where only the young survive, that she met my father, who was there on a business trip. He married her soon after, almost as one might acquire a trinket. I suspect he needed something pretty to dangle and she suited his purposes.

It was a whirlwind romance, conducted over half a year before he proposed and brought her back permanently as some exotic spoil. Although North America lacks the cultural ethos of Europe, my mother was never imaginative enough to miss what she had left behind. I gather it was more the lack of a bona fide class system and a sense of knowing one's place that she missed. She and my father seldom travelled after the marriage, but it turned out that she was the one who preferred to stay at home. He, on the other hand, continued his wanderings, and no doubt his flings as well, though I have to give him credit for not making the mistake of marrying any of the others if he did. He never tried to divorce my mother and she, for her part, kept silent about his affairs, if she suspected them. She was more inclined to enjoy her indolent lifestyle as a kept wife than gripe about his philandering, which would attest to the thick core of ice at her centre that always resists thawing.

Had I met either of them casually, at a club or some foreign café, I would not have given them a second glance. Is it ironic or just sad when we realize how little we have in common with our birth families? I've always believed the wisdom lay in accepting that fact rather than twisting oneself out of shape trying to change an unalterable part of our destiny in the hopes of pleasing someone who can never be pleased.

Lunch was nearly over and it seemed we had made it safely to the far shore as the waiters scurried about trying to satisfy her needs. I felt relaxed, though it may simply have been due to the second round of martinis. Despite my natural tendency toward caution and circumspection where my mother was concerned, I thought it time to come clean about what I was doing.

"You haven't really asked me about the job," I said.

Her eyes sparkled. "I didn't want to pry. I was waiting for you to tell me all about it when you felt ready."

My mother has always been an expert chess player. Even when she loses, she wins.

"I'm going to be working with victims of the Libyan Civil War, teaching them English while they're here for biomedical surgical procedures."

I was already becoming adept at the terminology, letting the words roll off my tongue as though I were entirely familiar with the operations my pupils were undergoing. My mother's face had taken on a clouded expression. Was it the mention of Libya or the war that had unsettled her?

"Are they soldiers?" she ventured hesitantly, as though testing the ice on treacherous shores with one foot before deciding whether to put her full weight on it.

"More or less. They call themselves Freedom Fighters. They became soldiers when they joined in the war. Most of them were ordinary citizens before that."

"On Mr. Gaddafi's side?" she suggested.

"No, I don't think so."

She hesitated, wiping her mouth with a napkin before speaking.

"He was very good to the British people. He gave us good, cheap oil. He was a very diplomatic man and a shrewd businessman. Quite civilized, I believe."

My mother is relentlessly cheerful. She could find the good in anyone: Caligula, Pol Pot, Herod the Great. Even Hitler might have been cause for cheer on a bad day.

"And that, in your estimation, makes him a good man?"

She eyed me for signs of insurrection. "He helped the kingdom, Geoffrey. One must know which side one is on. You can't hang back with the brutes."

"I suspect history will show Gaddafi to have been a tyrannical leader who routinely abused his subjects."

"I'm sure Mr. Gaddafi did the best he could under difficult circumstances."

I shook my head at this willful misapprehension of the facts. "He tortured and imprisoned his opponents. Does that make him civilized?"

She stared at me fiercely. "One must adapt," she snapped, as though explaining the facts of life to a half-wit.

"Adapt to what?" I asked, incredulous.

"He was no doubt being strategic. One hardly knows where to stand in difficult times. It was not that long ago he met with Prime Minister Blair, who declared it time for new relations between the two countries."

"Yes, because he sold off the oil fields. But of course that was years after the Lockerbie bombing, so no doubt he was a changed man by then."

My mother's brow contracted, as though she were having trouble recognizing the child she raised.

"Why must you be so unpleasant?"

I smiled. "One must adapt."

We finished our meal in silence. It was a protective shroud I had employed since childhood. It wasn't till we were headed back in the car that conversation resumed.

"We will have to visit your father's grave," she said at last.

"Yes, good idea," I concurred, safe in knowing it was a suggestion she frequently made at difficult moments, like a defeated general insisting on inspecting the troops, but one she seldom followed through on.

"When were you last there?" I asked.

"Last fall, I believe. I wanted to see how the stone was holding up."

While teaching in Croatia several years ago, I received an emailed photograph from my mother. It showed my father's gravestone adorned with a pair of praying hands. Why she chose that particular motif I can't say, as my father was not a religious man. His sole use for the church had been to further business efforts, expanding his clientele list via the socializing he did there, not to waste his time before, after, and probably even during the sermons. For some reason, my mother has kept up the fiction of his piety. Rather than a pair of hands, I think she should have had stock market quotations engraved on his marker. It would have suited him better.

"I'm thinking next Sunday from eleven-thirty to twelve noon," she said, as though she hoped to fit it in between a visit to the hairdresser and getting a manicure. "If you're free, of course. I don't want to interfere with your work schedule."

I assured her I would make the time, not wanting to put her off by reminding her my new job was a part-time gig that would take up no more than twenty hours a week at best.

"Structure," she called out after kissing my cheek and dropping me off in front of my apartment building.

I turned.

"Structure is good for you," she said with her relentless cheerfulness, as though offering an infallible recipe for success. "And of course punctuality. You'll see. This will be the making of you."

I smiled and waved goodbye as though all were well between us.

BODY/LANGUAGE

The following afternoon, my class consisted of just two students: Hassan and Abdel. The others were scheduled for appointments at the hospital and would rejoin us the following day. Although I'd been warned that disruptions of this nature were to be expected, I was disappointed not to see Yusuf again immediately.

While we managed to make some headway during our time together — young Hassan in particular seemed to warm to the lesson that day — I noted a marked inability on the part of both men to concentrate for prolonged periods of time. When their expressions glazed over in the middle of a sentence, as it often did, or if their gaze drifted to the windows overlooking the street, I simply asked what they were thinking about as a means of continuing our conversation. While I had expected to hear horrific stories of bloodshed and horizons stained by fighting, of the relentless fear that results from dodging bombs and bullets, or even of concern for their families, the answers were sometimes far simpler: worries about whether they had taken the correct medicine that morning or if they had missed a counseling session. Abdel, as always, was articulate and clever, though I could sense he was not as forthcoming with me as he might have been with someone he knew and trusted. Hassan, on the other hand, struggled with even the simplest English expressions, yet his ready smile told me he appreciated the efforts I was making for him.

While I found it difficult, I made a point of not feeling sorry for these men, both of whom were facing the inescapable prospects of a life of reduced mobility. I knew only their current reality. I had no idea what their lives had been like back in Libya. Were they poor or rich? Did they live in houses where such basic issues as accessibility could be easily mastered when they returned to them or was that simply a First World concept? I thought of the audio signals installed at major intersections around the city, the beeping sounds that enable the visually impaired to cross in safety. Did such things exist outside a small bubble of privilege in North America and Europe?

To get him to focus, I asked Abdel about his farming and his family. He was forthcoming on both subjects. He needed minimal instruction and was quick to pick up on my suggestions on how he could improve his vocabulary and pronunciation. With all of my students, but with these men in particular, I became adept at assessing their frame of mind each time we met, knowing whether it was a day to push forward or simply try to be good company and encourage as much conversation as they could manage. Clearly, with the war so recent and their injuries so severe, they were still adjusting psychologically and emotionally to all that had happened to them.

While Abdel could be gruff, and wore a brutish look, I sensed the soul of a sensitive man. I felt he was just trying to make the best of his opportunities, both medical and educational, knowing his time was limited. He missed his family, he said.

"Two girls and a boy," he replied when I asked.

I assumed there was a wife in the picture, though clearly the children were his pride.

"Who is the oldest?" I asked.

"Aliya." He smiled briefly then a moment later turned away with tears in his eyes.

"I'm sorry," I said. "Would you rather change the subject?"

"I miss them," he said simply, quickly composing himself.

Along with their injuries, I constantly had to remind myself, these men were also dealing with cultural adjustment. Estranged from their lives and families, ensconced in a foreign country with only a small band of fellow countrymen for company, it was obvious that nothing about their existence could be easy. Part of my job was to make it so. I realized I had much to learn when it came to dealing with pupils like these.

Hassan hid whatever sensitivity he had behind those beautiful eyes and their thick lashes. His expression was soulful, like the face of a martyr in some medieval painting. He also had the advantage of knowing so little English that he could easily pretend not to understand if I or any of the others said anything that disturbed him. I suspect he took refuge in that tactic from time to time.

There was no official textbook for the course. I relied largely on conversational English to teach these men. My approach was pragmatic: I would provide them with a basic grasp of the language in everyday usage, enabling them to better communicate their needs outside the small world of the hotel and hospital and in their interactions with others in the program. Initially, I concentrated on a vocabulary focusing on food, medical terms and directions — things they would find useful. To augment this, I occasionally brought in a poem or short news article to acquaint them with the appearance of letters on the page, the English alphabet being so different in appearance from the Arabic. I find it often helps students to visualize the words, providing a firmer grasp on the division between syllables in this tricky, knotty language of ours. With more accomplished students, I also set pronunciation quizzes.

To help students understand the difficulties English posed, I might ask, "How do you pronounce the letters g-h-o-t-i?"

I always wrote it in large letters and held the paper up in front of them. Attempts were made, often reasonable enough, but I would smile and wipe them all away.

"No," was always my reply. "It spells *fish*."

Incredulous, they would stare at me, demanding an explanation.

"G-h as in *enough*," I would say, waiting till they grasped the concept. "O as in *women*." I would nod to encourage them as they got the joke. "And t-i as in *attention*. That spells *fish*. And that is the perverse nature of the English language, a tongue that steals from every other language so routinely and deftly that all rules of pronunciation are to be considered suspect."

If nothing else, it made my students stop and consider the immense possibilities, as well as the difficulties, of learning a new tongue and perhaps realize that, like life, languages are never simple to master.

Yusuf continued to be a problem as far as punctuality was concerned. He was late for our next two sessions, disrupting the class with his entrance, despite appearing genuinely contrite. I wondered if he was avoiding any chance of a private confrontation with me, always making sure he arrived after the others, or if he simply wasn't interested in the lessons, though he clearly applied himself when we were all together. I reminded myself of Marcus's admonition that the medication made it difficult for these men to navigate their daily lives with the focus it required. In class, Yusuf was polite but guarded in response to any personal questions I directed to him. The clownish side of him that I had first encountered seemed to have disappeared. Perhaps he was wary of revealing too much of himself.

So far there had been no acknowledgment by either of us of our near encounter at the bar. I didn't feel it was up to me to bring the matter up, especially considering our present teacher-pupil relationship. As well, I had to remind myself, I had no idea of the social world he came from. Perhaps any overt acknowledgement of such things would prove disastrous for him, which in the end is precisely what happened.

On the third day, he simply didn't show up for the session. I called the number Marcus had given me, but there was no answer. I phoned Marcus to let him know of Yusuf's absence. While I waited, I could hear him checking his records. After a moment, he was back on the phone.

"Sorry, Yusuf is scheduled for a doctor's appointment this afternoon. I should have let you know."

He thanked me for my persistence in checking with him. I hung up feeling oddly disappointed that I would not see what I had come to think of as my most intriguing pupil that day.

The next day Yusuf was again a no-show, this time for our scheduled one-on-one session. I called his room, but there was no answer. The same went for his cell. I was going to leave it at that, but curiosity got the better of me. As I had no other lessons scheduled that afternoon, I got in the elevator and rode it upstairs.

Yusuf's room was on the sixteenth floor. I knocked cautiously on his door. There was no response. I called his cell again and was surprised to hear a distinctive Middle-Eastern ring tone coming from inside the room. After a moment, I heard someone clumsily moving about. The door opened and Yusuf peered out. All was dark behind him.

"Yes?" he said, squinting at me.

"I'm sorry for disturbing you, Yusuf, but it's time for our lesson."

He shook his head. It took a second for my words to register.

"Ah, yes! English tutor. Come in, please."

He opened the door. I followed and stood inside the entry. He was dressed in a striped dressing gown, his hair tumbling over his shoulders. I watched as he rubbed his forehead and picked up a small medicine vial from the bedside table. He shook it.

"Take many," he said.

He still seemed in a fog.

"Would you like some coffee?" I suggested.

"Yes. This good."

"I'll be right back," I assured him.

I went down to the lobby café and soon returned bearing a steaming cup of the strongest coffee available. Yusuf had combed his hair and put on a T-shirt and grey sweatpants by then. I held out the cup and watched as he reached with both hands to grip it. The left one was swathed in bandages.

"*Chokron*," he said.

"You are welcome, Yusuf."

He looked at me then laughed.

"I speak Arabic to you."

"It's okay, I understood."

He took a gulp of coffee then lay back on the bed, closing his eyes. He opened them again suddenly.

"Sorry, sorry … my head is like … night."

I nodded and pulled a chair up beside him. He sat up and took another sip, struggling to set the cup on his bedside table. I reached out instinctively to help as he fumbled it toward the surface.

"No." He shook his head. "I do."

"All right."

He picked up the pill bottle again, unscrewed the top and shook the remnants into his hand.

"No enough," he said woefully.

"They didn't give you enough medicine?"

"No." He shook his head again. "I take many. Sleep then wake up. Take many again. One day so many. Not good."

I glimpsed his meaning. "You woke up and took more because you forgot you already took your medicine?"

"Yes! I am stupid for this."

He hit the side of his head with his bandaged hand. I cringed.

"Careful," I said.

He looked at me oddly, as though it seemed peculiar that I

should care.

"Yes, okay."

I watched as he opened a drawer beside his bed, his fingers passing over a collection of bottles containing a cornucopia of pills of different shapes and colors. It would be a challenge for anyone to remember which pill was to be taken when, not to mention whether it was to be taken before, during or after meals. He picked up two vials, shaking his head as he read the labels aloud then let them drop again. The third one seemed to be what he was searching for. He opened it, shook two pills into his hand and swallowed them.

"I can get you a pill dispenser."

He stared at me blankly.

"It's a container with a section for each day of the week," I explained. "That way you will know if you took your pills already. You understand?"

"This true? You do this for Yusuf?"

"Yes, of course," I said. "Then you will always remember to take your medicine properly."

"You are good man, Geef!"

His mispronunciation of my name was endearing. I didn't correct him.

"Tomorrow," I said. "I'll have it for you tomorrow when you come to class."

He went to the window and pulled the curtains aside, letting in a stream of light. I watched as he wandered out onto the balcony, leaning unsteadily to look at the ground below as he drank his coffee. I felt a surge of nausea seeing him hang there sixteen floors up before he turned around and came back in.

The caffeine was having an effect on him. His expression was more alive and alert than it had been when I arrived. It occurred to me we might just as easily hold our session there in his hotel room. When he agreed, I pulled up a chair and sat facing him on the bed. I found him forthcoming about subjects of personal interest, particularly the civil war that had helped unseat the dictator Gaddafi.

"I am Freedom Fighter!" he proclaimed, when I asked what he did back home.

"But as the war is now over, that would make you an ex-Freedom Fighter," I explained pedantically.

He stared uncomprehendingly. "This Yusuf," he stated, his brow creased with consternation. "This me."

I did not elaborate. Sometimes subtleties get the better of even the best students, proving time-consuming and meaningless to explain, and at that moment Yusuf seemed hardly the best of students. "What did you do before the war?"

"Before?" he repeated with a confused expression, as though he could not recall a time before the conflict.

"Prior to. In the past. What did you do?"

"Ah, yes! I am medical student," he explained to my surprise. "I drive ambulance for war."

"You drove an ambulance in the war?" I asked, hoping I understood correctly that he was in actuality one of the peacemakers rather than a killer, however noble or legitimate the cause.

"Yes, I am medic." He held up his left hand, showing me the bandaged stubs of his missing fingers. "I lose my hand."

"I *lost* my hand," I corrected, instantly regretting my tactlessness.

I noticed a change in his expression. He stared at me as if to gauge whether I could possibly comprehend such a thing from my privileged position in the world.

"I *lost* my hand," he repeated.

"I'm sorry," I said.

"Is no problem." He shrugged off my apology then added coyly, "Teacher is boss."

I nodded. "Yes, teacher is boss."

I glanced at my watch. With the lesson's aborted beginning, our hour was nearly up. "I should go," I said.

He continued to stare at me.

"I like you, Geef," he said simply.

"I like you too, Yusuf," I said. "You're a good student."

What he did next caught me totally by surprise. As he stood up nimbly from the bed, planting himself squarely before me, his sweatpants tented with a noticeable erection. How he had sat there like that without my noticing it was beyond me.

"Yes, I like you," he repeated breathily, placing his left hand — his damaged hand — on my head.

With his right hand, he untied the knot in his sweats and let them fall to the floor. His erection dangled before me like ripe fruit, dark and swollen. The action was so deftly performed we might have been in a porn movie.

His hand guided my head forward.

"You are nice teacher for Yusuf."

Without stopping to think what I was getting into, I took him in my mouth. He pumped urgently, like a man starved for sex. Yet it seemed almost as though there was nothing carnal or lustful about his actions. It was simply a physical function — a bodily exertion ending in a release — as basic as pissing or shitting.

When he was done, he reached over and pulled a Kleenex from a box then wiped himself off and bundled himself back inside his pants. He didn't offer me a tissue or ask about my pleasure. These things seemed to be of no interest to him.

I sat there, a little stunned by what had just happened. A myriad random thoughts were going through my head. Would he tell anyone? Had I just lost my job? What in the world was I thinking letting him do this to me?

"You like this fun?" he asked, as he finished retying the knot on his pants with no difficulty despite his handicap.

My sense of irony suddenly reasserted itself.

"It was fine. You're a beautiful specimen. It wasn't quite the hospitality I was expecting, though."

He looked at me balefully. "Sorry, Geef, this too fast me to understand."

"That's all right." I nodded. "Yes, I liked it."

"Good." He smiled. "When I see teacher I say, 'I want this.'"

"'Him'," I corrected. "I want *him*."

"Yes," he repeated. "I want *him*."

He stood gazing down at me. He was handsome in a hard-looking way, what my friends would have called *rough trade*, the implication being that a little danger had its appeal. The shock of our encounter had already passed. I was fully aroused now, but it was clear the episode was over for him. He put his right hand over his heart.

"We are same-same. You are best for me," he said in such a serious tone I almost laughed. "You don't speak Marcus this fun, no?"

I shook my head, relieved by his words. "No," I agreed. "I won't tell Marcus about our fun."

He smiled. "*Chokron.*" He repeated the gesture of hand over heart. "I sleep good now."

He lay back on the bed and pulled the covers over him. His eyes quickly closed and a rhythmic breathing took over his body. I sat there for a while watching him, drinking in his physical splendor, then let myself out of the room and crept silently down the hall.

DAVID

He eyed me over a cappuccino from behind reflective sunglasses. A little greyer on top and a lot heavier in the middle now. I still remembered him as a relatively slim guy, a loud personality behind the ticket booth at the Winter Garden Theatre, a walking encyclopedia of the stage and a talker so mesmerizing as to make our first meeting unforgettable more than a decade later.

Since my return, David and I had been seeing a good deal of one another. Apart from what I considered time wasted at the bars, he was my only reprieve from the loneliness and boredom that were my constant companions outside of work. Afternoons we whiled away gossiping and kvetching at some coffee house on the strip; evenings we spent with a drink or over a game of pool. Talk was a constant, and David's tongue was never idle when there was a quip to be made or an observation to share. He was one of my few before-and-after friends, our camaraderie having survived the years I spent away from the city and the concomitant changes to our lives. We had met up twice in Europe during my exile, but on my return it was as if no time had passed. It felt reassuring to know some things endured its tortuous flow.

David's mind tends to move at warp speed, one of the

reasons I never got bored with him. Over the years it was I who made the effort to keep in touch, relishing his observations on cultural matters as well as those of a more personal nature. His insights into relationships were always surprisingly sophisticated — and far deeper — than any Miss Manners-style columnist or guest therapist on *Oprah*. And that is not meant ironically. David's assessments of the emotional intricacies of the heart are peerless, despite the fact that he considers himself an outcast from the realms of romance. I had often confided my concerns about whatever relationship I was then currently in, knowing he would nail it to the wall within a minute or two.

"You know what your problem is…?" he would begin, after I had explained the ins and outs of my current amorous alliance.

"No, that's why I'm asking you."

And then he would tell me exactly what was wrong, outlining both my side and the other person's without ever having met the Man of the Hour.

"He's a narcissist," he would say, enlightening me as to why a current boyfriend always told me in detail how he was feeling, but never took the time to ask about me in return. "He probably never thinks about it. How you feel is immaterial as long as you make him happy. He wants things focused on himself. When you stop playing along and stop telling him he's Mr. Wonderful, then he'll drop you."

I took his advice and found myself dropped in a matter of weeks, with the parting adage, "You've changed, Geoff."

David's pronouncements proved true time and again.

"Time to find someone who respects your opinions," he said of another boyfriend who had constantly disregarded my advice concerning his ex-wife, whose unreasonable demands to look after their son constantly disrupted our time together. "He feels guilty for leaving her and probably for being gay as well, because it means he was lying the whole time he was with her. But he doesn't want you to solve his problems or else he would take your advice to ignore her. He just wants you to sympathize, which means he will probably never confront her."

Right again. I was in awe of his ability to explain my conundrums while viewing them at a distance.

"That is precisely why I can see them better than you can. You wear your emotions on your sleeve. You can't step aside from them."

"So why are you perpetually single?" I asked. "You're the Genius of Love."

"I'm also a creature of habit," he told me. "I keep repeating the same deadly patterns. I am perpetually attracted to men who like me for a bit of fun — a daddy figure, if you will — but not enough to stick around long enough to bring out my domestic side. I also don't respect my own genius, as you call it. I never take my own advice. It just seems too simple."

He fixed his gaze on me now. The subject was Yusuf.

"Have you had sex with him yet?" he asked, then made a frenzied motion with his hands as though to erase the very words. "Wait! What am I saying? Of course you have. You're a lonely gay man and he's a wounded boy. It would be impossible for you to resist him and he knows that. So he pounced. And you didn't resist, did you?"

I shook my head. "It was over before I had time to figure out what was happening. I've never experienced anything that was quite so literally, 'Wham, bam, thank you Sam.'"

"By which I conclude he must also be good-looking and sexy as hell," David continued, though I hadn't yet described Yusuf's physical attributes.

"You're right. He is both, but how do you figure that?"

"Because I know you. You never make the first move. And he would have to be very confident that you would go for him, ergo he must be attractive despite his handicaps."

"Right again," I admitted. "He's stunning in a raw, sensual way. It doesn't hurt that he's still in his twenties and fit as can be. Despite his injury, he drips sex appeal."

"It all contributes to the sympathy factor." David shook his head like a mother sorely disappointed by her progeny yet again. "Boyo, you sure can attract them. I hope you know that all these stray cats and dogs you keep bringing home are going to cost you one day."

He had never been so accurate as he was at that moment.

"Question is, what am I going to do with him?"

David gave me a knowing look. "You're going to enjoy him while he's in your hands and then wish him well when they ship him back to Liberia or wherever he comes from."

"Libya."

David shrugged. "Wherever. It doesn't matter. He doesn't belong here. Just remember that and don't let me hear you fooling yourself about it in future."

I shivered to hear those words. David's insight had proved uncanny yet again. I'd already begun to fantasize something longer term between us, hot and sexy and dripping with passion till we were both eighty or more. It was every gay man's dream relationship. I was far from being sexually naïve, but what I'd experienced with Yusuf was so raw, so thrilling, that it had begun to seep into my daydreams and threatened to turn into my next obsession.

"I won't," I promised.

"I hope not." He took off his glasses and fixed me with a shrewd gaze. "These things never last. Tell me you know that."

"I know that."

"Now tell me everything you know about him and I'll tell you all the reasons he's wrong for you."

I laughed. "I need fuel before I answer. Let's grab a bite somewhere."

Fifteen minutes later we were at Pergola, just down the street. We ensconced ourselves in lounge chairs in front of a gas fireplace. It was cozy. David shook his head when the waiter came by to take our order.

"Just tea for me," he said.

I looked at him. "Really?"

He patted his stomach. "Got to trim down a little," he told me. "It's been affecting my ankle."

To see him now, you would never believe David had been a highly paid go-go boy at the age of twenty-nothing, dancing in one of the city's busiest nightclubs, suspended high above the dance floor in a gilded cage, always partnered with go-go girls. Leather and lace, and all of them Broadway bound, if you asked them about their dreams. Then, at twenty-three, he broke his ankle roller-blading. It was a bad break. No more dancing, no more career. He cut his hair, bought a conservative-looking suit and took up bookkeeping, like some alter-ego transformation, becoming a Stepford accountant.

I scarcely needed reminding that all our younger selves are buried somewhere beneath their older incarnations. For David the weight came quickly, almost in revenge, and never went away. He claimed not to mind but for the physical inconvenience it brought on.

"So — tell all. What do you know about him?"

"Not very much. He was a medical student before the war, just a few months shy of finishing his degree. Then, like a lot of other idealists, he became a Freedom Fighter helping to liberate his country. He was at Gaddafi's palace when the walls came tumbling down."

"He's earned his place in history then. He's probably proud of it, too."

I recalled how eagerly Yusuf had told me of his part in the war: *This Yusuf. This me.*

"But a soldier?" David shot me a cautionary look to be sure I was heeding his words. "That can't be good. He kills people for a living. Who knows what brutal passions lurk inside his savage breast."

"It's not like that," I protested. "He was one of thousands — hundreds of thousands — of civilians who rose up against a tyrannical dictator. Think of it — all those ordinary people wanting a better way of life, rising up against tyranny."

"Yeah — that's what the Americans said when they rebelled against King George III, but they were really just pissed about the taxes."

I gave him a sour look.

He shrugged. "Continue."

"Actually, he wasn't a soldier in the war. He was an ambulance driver. I think he just likes calling himself a Freedom Fighter. It has a heroic ring."

"Yes, I see." David nodded sagely. "Ambulance driver is better."

"I think he's a genuinely good person," I said. "Think of it. If it were you and me and the government here suddenly went completely fascist—"

"As opposed to the half-assed fascists they are currently pretending not to be?"

"Right. Wouldn't we both join in the revolution to overthrow a corrupt government?"

"You might, because you have scruples. I would probably just wait it out and hope the good guys won." He shrugged. "But you've got a point. What's the joy in living under tyranny? Big zero."

"That's what I'm saying. Yusuf made a choice, but his choice was to further the revolution in a non-violent way."

"Congratulations." David smiled. "You just made him into a martyr-hero."

"I did, didn't I?"

The waiter arrived with our drinks. David thanked him and sent him on his way then turned back to me.

"What you need to remember is that he comes from a world of war and unpredictability. You need to consider his mindset. He will more than likely wear that mentality along with all his emotional baggage for the rest of his life. Does he even know what being gay means?"

"What do you mean?" I asked, suddenly feeling

uncomfortable.

"It means he may never see the world the way you or I see it. To us it's a Land of Plenty, a Land of Opportunity. Ask and it shall be given. You want to be gay, then be gay. You want to be rich, then get a job. But not everyone who comes here fits in. It's the mindset that determines how you see your life. My father had no problem making money when he arrived here. He worked hard and became a success, but in his mind he never left Italy. He is still that small-minded *paisano* he was when he arrived here at the age of nineteen with a sixteen-year-old bride. His outlook never changed. If you don't like something, you get angry and yell. And if you get something good then you hide it before someone else steals it. It's a bleak outlook, but after forty-five years in this country he hasn't softened or changed in the slightest."

"Sounds harsh."

"It is." David shrugged and sipped his tea. "As I said, enjoy the sex. You need that to be happy now that you've lost Europe," he declared, making it sound like a game of *Risk*. "Just remember not to get carried away with dreams of happily-ever-after. These things never work out in the way you think they're going to."

Unparalleled words of wisdom, had I only listened to them.

VULNERABLE

Now that I was busy with work, I found it easier to resist the temptation to go out on the town every night. I was no longer restless, no longer susceptible to the tidal surges drawing me away from the narrow shores of my life. Instead, I lay in bed for hours turning the pages of books while fantasizing about Yusuf, thinking how I would teach him English and help him find a job and settle here permanently. I'd longed for a reason to stop going out to the bars, drawn like some doomed insect to the false lights that blinded me; suddenly I had one.

Reading kept my interest now, whereas earlier it had seemed a tiresome distraction. A biography of Proust currently held my attention. The previous year, while teaching in Paris, I'd made it through all seven volumes of his tale of obsessive love, surprised by how many times I saw myself in those pages of overwrought prose, yet how often I found myself thinking I would have written it exactly that way. The life story of a neurotic, asthmatic, homosexual writer should not have been as gripping as it was, but nevertheless it kept me rapt for hours, reminding me of those leisurely Parisian days when I had felt young and carefree. When I wasn't reading I occasionally turned on the television, trying to outwit Sherlock Holmes and arrive at the solution to impossible mysteries before Benedict

Cumberbatch's nimble insights shattered my facile conclusions again and again.

Although it was much easier to stay at home, it did little to assuage my loneliness or bring relief to the hours of darkness haunting me. Apart from my daily calls to David, there was virtually no one else in the city I felt a desire to talk to, no one to share my hidden vulnerabilities and ravenous emotional needs. My mother? Not on your life. And certainly not my father, even when he was alive. My sexuality was something we discussed once and left bleeding on the battlefield, a no-man's land that none dared approach. In my father's eyes, anyone who *chose* to lead a queer lifestyle, as I apparently had, could not hope to make a difference in the world at large. I was a broken branch on the family tree, a shameful secret tolerated but never discussed, like some mad Victorian relative kept hidden in the attic. I discovered as much at his sixty-fifth birthday party the year before he died. On arriving at my parents' house I walked into a room full of strangers, mostly self-made businessmen and CEOs, all impressed with their might and financial worth. I soon found myself thinking: there but for the grace of an intransigent personality go I. Nevertheless, I dutifully made the rounds of people gathered in my father's honor and quickly discerned that I neither liked them nor wanted to get to know them better.

A jolly-looking man with the reddened cheeks of a practiced drinker intercepted me at the bar.

"Clay Wilson, head of sales at IBM," he informed me, his hand held out. "I'm George's best friend. Who are you?"

"I'm the long-lost son," I replied. "The heir unapparent."

He stared as though I were a deranged person who was threatening to take a swing at him.

"I never knew George had a son," he said, blinking and looking stunned as he scanned his memory for evidence of my prior existence.

"Please don't say anything. No one here knows," I replied conspiratorially. "I'm not sure he knows himself."

I tipped my glass and wandered off, wondering what Clay would tell my father the next time he got him alone. Perhaps he would mention the delusional young man he'd encountered spreading lies about his paternity.

But my father was gone now and my mother and I rarely agreed on anything important, so there was no one else to call when I felt the crushing weight of loneliness. Over the years, almost all of my old friends had settled down, married and had children, no longer quite as fond of seeing me as they had been in the days of our carefree youth. On the surface, at least, I was still a free man, but ironically they were not. I think it grated on them.

My European idylls were also of the past and did not look as though they would return any time soon. Memories were best kept for happier moments, I found. Dreaming of long-ago pleasantries would only lead to further melancholy.

Instead, I turned my thoughts to Yusuf. For the past few days I'd replayed our sexual encounter over and over again in my mind until it had taken on the importance of an event akin to losing one's virginity. I knew I was tempting fate when I pulled out the sheets Marcus had given me outlining the personal information of each student. Don't be afraid to get to know them, he'd said. They're just men, like us.

I wondered how much voyeuristic thinking had been behind that statement. Suddenly my mind did a double-take. Had Marcus too had sexual encounters with Yusuf? The thought intrigued me. I pictured the two of them coupling: the thin, nervous Marcus bottoming with the energetic and muscular Yusuf topping him. Without realizing it, I'd given myself an erection. I shook myself free of the thoughts. Not my finest hour as a tutor, but hell, I was human.

I turned my attention back to the sheets. There was Yusuf's name in black and white. I stared at it as a vision of his face hovered before me, tantalizing, hanging in the air. That was all it took. The memory of his sexual vibrancy filled me. It was a little after nine o'clock. I picked up my cell and dialed.

His phone rang somewhere on the other end, but he didn't pick up. I hung up, thankful for having been spared the embarrassment of having to explain why I'd called so late. I tried to imagine what he might be up to. After all, he lived in a large hotel where there were endless diversions. Perhaps he was in the bar downstairs. Then I remembered that Muslims don't drink alcohol.

I put my phone down and picked up the Proust, but suddenly found I had lost all interest in the story of a neurotic, under-sexed, turn-of-the-previous-century Parisian. His life may have provided him with fodder for a five-thousand-page opus, but I had problems of my own, the primary one being loneliness.

I nearly jumped when the phone rang.

"Hello?"

"This Yusuf."

My heart leaped into my throat. "Hello, Yusuf," I said, trying to sound in control of my voice. "This is your English tutor."

"Hello, Geef," he said. His voice was dull and lethargic. Perhaps I had woken him up.

"How are you, Yusuf?" I asked.

"Yusuf good. I am at gym sauna."

My mind leapt at the possibilities.

"I see number for Geef. I think Geef need Yusuf."

"Yes," I said, not wanting to admit how close to home his words were. "I just wanted to make sure everything is okay with you." Did I sound believable? How transparent could I be without scaring him off? "How is your medication coming along?"

I had bought a pill dispenser and given it to him the day after our conversation, but hadn't heard from him since.

"Is good," he replied. "Not more so many pills. Thank you for present."

"I'm very glad to hear it. Is there anything else I can do for you?"

"Geef," he said hesitantly, the silence hanging heavily on the line.

I waited anxiously. I was half-expecting him to say that what we had done the other day was not to be repeated, reproaching us both for our bad behavior. Good Muslims, his silence seemed to be saying, did not engage in homosexual practice. It was against Sharia Law. I was preparing an apology in my head, claiming full responsibility as both his teacher and the older partner involved. It was up to me to point it out.

[61]

"Geef, I like you."

I trembled at his words. "I like you, too, Yusuf."

"Please, can you coming?"

"You want me to come to the hotel?"

"Yes, Geef." His tone was urgent, passionate. "Please. You are best for me."

An electric current flowed through me. I looked at my watch. It was just before nine-thirty.

"Yes, I can be there by ten."

"Come, Geef. Please. Yusuf need you."

I had no illusions after my talk with David. I knew this boy was trouble, pure and simple, but my mind was on fire as I showered and dressed to meet him. I had been feeling old. I'd felt myself confronting that long, inexorable slide into middle age and everything it entailed, aware there was no turning back. Suddenly, I longed to break the mirror's spell and whatever hold it had over me.

I took a cab to the hotel and stood outside the entrance looking up. I pictured him waiting alone in his room for me. This, I knew, was how obsessions started: with a deep hunger for someone you knew was all wrong for you. The rest would work itself out through whatever punishment had been predetermined for wrong-headed love affairs since the beginning of time. This couldn't happen, I told myself. This was not wise, not smart, not good. But I wanted him so badly I could not have stopped myself from passing through the revolving doors, getting into the elevator and punching the button for the sixteenth floor.

The hallway seemed interminably long. Supply carts stacked with linen and toiletries were parked outside rooms alongside room service trays, their contents picked clean and the dishes sent back whence they came. Finally, I reached his door and knocked. He answered, once again wearing only the dressing gown he had worn the afternoon of our encounter. This time there was no guessing at one another's intentions. The door closed and we were in each other's arms, kissing fiercely, hungrily. I felt his hard-on pressing against my abdomen as his gown fell to the floor.

He pushed me to my knees.

"Please, Geef. Yusuf need you."

There was no subtlety in his approach. I gathered that unless I turned the tide, and soon, this would simply be a repeat of our initial engagement.

"Not like this," I said, rising. "I want to see you. I want to feel you."

It took him only a moment to comprehend my words.

"Geef, you like to fuck?"

It did not escape my attention that he seemed to have a command of pertinent elements of the English language. I nodded and quickly removed my clothes then lay on my back while he straddled me. Once again, there was no foreplay, just straight to the act.

"Wait!" I cried as his erection probed indelicately between my legs. "What about a condom?"

"Why need condom?"

"To be safe," I said, a little taken aback. "To protect against HIV."

"But this for gays," he said, as though somehow we were both exempt from the category. David's warning rang sharply in my head.

"In North America," I said, "we always use condoms."

He shrugged. Yanking open the bedside drawer with his good hand, he extracted a green and silver square, ripped it open with his teeth and slipped the rubber over his cock.

Before I could say "not too fast," he was inside me. I gasped at the intrusion. It had been a while, but I quickly got past the awkward burning that precedes the more agreeable sensation. I lay back, mesmerized by his animal-like absorption in the task. He was extremely agile, considering he had only one good hand. It struck me in that moment how extraordinary our coupling was. I couldn't recall the last time I'd had sex that wasn't attempting in one way or another to reproduce the simulated excitement of a porn film. My generation had been groomed on sex videos. Like trained seals, we expected just so much foreplay, just so much oral and anal stimulation, followed by perfectly-timed ejaculations, preferably visible from all camera angles. But this wasn't a choreographed dance or an acrobatic routine. It was pure, raw attraction. And this time both of us came. Yusuf had taken me and my libido by complete surprise before, but now I was ready. It was the most satisfying sex I'd had in years.

Afterwards he sprawled beside me, spewing those nonsense phrases he had obviously cultivated for post-coital conversation.

"Geef, you are my best. You are my lovely. I like you, Geef."

Suddenly, he stood and went to the washroom, leaving

the door open. I watched as he went through the ritual of meticulously washing his genitals, like a good workman cleaning his tools after a hard day's work. He emerged and glanced over to where I lay on the bed.

"Geef, need to wash."

He nodded to the bathroom. I went in, took a quick shower and returned. He watched appreciatively as I toweled myself off.

"You are sexy man," he said. "I like you."

"Thanks," I said. "*Chokron.*"

He laughed at my use of Arabic as he pulled on a pair of sweatpants and T-shirt then sat cross-legged on the bed. I watched while he turned to the pill dispenser I'd given him, unsnapping a single lid before swallowing several colored capsules, followed by a long gulp of water from a glass on the bedside table. Next he performed some prayer-like ablutions in which I heard the word Allah repeated several times. After that, I expected him to lie back and pull the covers up then dismiss me as he had the other day. Instead, he looked up at me and smiled.

"You can to sleeping with Yusuf?" he asked gently. He raised the covers invitingly. "Please, Geef," he said, his eyes begging me to join him.

I got in. Without further conversation, he turned out the light. Instinctively, I grappled him from behind, pressing my face against his back, our legs intertwined. The palm of my hand cupped his navel, pulling him in to me. He was still *terra incognita,* an unexplored land, but it already felt like we'd been doing this for years, the intimacy between us complete. It would be our favored sleeping position, with me the protector and him the treasure to be guarded with all my might, for the rest of our short time together.

SHOPPING

Morning crept into the room, lighting up Yusuf's profile on the pillow, his hair splayed out around him. His was a beauty that burned. Not radiantly, as in romantic novels, but harshly, like something to watch out for lest it get too close and consume you in turn. The haunted look that emanated from his eyes said he had seen too much. He was the sort of man wise parents would have told their daughters to beware of. I readily admit that I saw it from the start. But I, eschewer of all conventional wisdom, paid no attention to those whispered warnings. It wouldn't have mattered where they came from. Not even David could have turned me from him.

All night long, as I slept and woke beside him, I replayed over and over again in my mind all the reasons I should not be there: I was his teacher and he was younger than me; he was a victim of war and I an indolent adherent of pleasure; he came from a culture and a religion that abhorred what I represented, both sexually and morally. We weren't even remotely Romeo and Juliet, breaking prohibitions on a family feud. Rather, we were Romeo and Othello lying together in unnatural wedlock, a queer connubial bliss making the beast with two backs while waiting for our Iago to come and betray us. In fact, our Iago would come, as he had to, his treachery precipitating all that happened afterward. But for that solitary moment, as Yusuf lay sleeping in my arms, I watched him in all his wounded beauty and fought to hold onto those brief hours as though I could make them last forever.

David had been right: I was already deluding myself, making Yusuf into something he wasn't. It was clear he knew me far too well, perhaps even better than I knew myself. Not only my tendency to romanticize and fantasize, but my unwillingness to stop doing so, flying headlong into the face of the unknown, in whatever guise I might find it, so desperate was I to belong somewhere.

In the morning I got up, opened the curtains and stood looking out at the rain. It drenched the streets below and obliterated the horizon. The high-rises surrounding the hotel were uniform: one wall of all-blue curtains, another of all-white curtains. I imagined every room being exactly alike inside: boring and stultifying, like so much of my life since my return. I didn't care. For once I had everything I needed inside a tiny rectangle of concrete walls and carpeted floor.

It was early. I went back to the bed and shook Yusuf, but he didn't move. I turned on the television, but he still didn't wake. After ten minutes, he opened one groggy eye and stared at me as though he couldn't quite place this strange man in his room. He nodded to the dresser where his room pass lay.

"If need go, take it."

He fell back asleep.

I showered and went out for coffee. Saturday morning was asserting itself, the Yonge Street strip coming alive. When I left the country nearly a decade earlier, the city had seemed like one of the sleepiest backwaters you could imagine. It felt like an insecure person seeking approval from everyone it encountered, whereas now it bustled and hurried along with no regard for anyone else.

I took great care leaving Yusuf's room, peering up and down the corridor before stepping into the hallway. As it turned out, I needn't have been so cautious. It was a big hotel, with many guests. One person in a hundred isn't going to stand out, and anyway I had a legitimate excuse for being there, even if it wasn't actually a teaching day.

I went out for breakfast, lingered over coffee, watched people check their cell phones and gulp food all around me, anxious to get on with their day. Even inside the walls of a small diner, it felt like I was living in a large metropolis. The city had transformed itself.

After I'd finished eating, I ordered a bagel and egg sandwich to go, trying to recall Yusuf's dietary proscriptions. The waiter brown-bagged it for me and I left.

When I returned, Yusuf was just getting out of bed. He was still groggy.

He blinked away the sleep on seeing me. "Geef, good dreams."

"You had good dreams last night?"

"Yes."

He smiled at me as though I were personally responsible for this. Had I known about the mostly unchecked nightmares he'd been having since the war, I would have realized that this was not only unusual, but also significant as regards his emotional state.

"What did you dream about?"

"Yusuf and Geef in olive garden. Geef kill scorpion," he continued. "Make Yusuf safe."

Now it was my turn to smile.

"I killed a scorpion and saved you?"

"Yes."

I had assumed the role of hero-protector in his eyes: *Teacher is boss.*

"Breakfast?" I suggested, holding out the highly aromatic sack I'd brought back from the restaurant.

Yusuf's face contorted. He rubbed his stomach.

"I cannot. Medication too strong in morning."

"No problem," I said.

I set the bag on his dresser, hoping he would remember it before it went bad.

I had no lessons scheduled that day, no place I had to be. I wondered just how far to push my desire for companionship. Yusuf seemed in no hurry for me to leave, though I had no idea what his days consisted of. Did he have a round of medical checkups scheduled or did he just lie about in a drug-induced haze, turning to television as a way of passing the hours, conscripted by his body's healing? I thought of my own impatience with illness of any sort, how I would do almost anything to avoid having to lie in bed when I could be out doing something, even if it delayed the healing.

He stood and stretched, letting his hair fall free. His body was leonine, his muscles taut and sinewy. I felt my desire for him flare. I had the urge to grapple him and bring him to the floor, to quench my arousal then and there. Long ago I had learned that sexual urges do not remain at a fever pitch in any relationship, so it's better to indulge them when you can rather than wait for time to bring about their eventual dissolution.

After that, as David always pointed out, it takes more than physical appeal to keep a relationship intact. You need to have things in common. Was there even the slightest chance Yusuf and I might have things in common twenty years from now? Or even five? My doubts suggested otherwise.

"Do you want me to leave so you can get on with your day?"

He stared at me a moment, digesting the words.

"You want leave?"

"No." I shook my head. "I can stay if you like."

"Please, Geef. Stay with Yusuf."

I nodded. I was beginning to see that his need for company might even exceed my own, his empty hours equal to mine, both of us struggling to fill them with meaningful activity.

"Okay. What would you like to do?"

His eyes lit up. He smiled like a boy being offered a treat.

"Geef, I like to shopping."

"Then let's shop!" I said, so overjoyed for any reason to spend time with him that I didn't bother to correct his grammar.

Shopping with Yusuf turned out to entail a tour of his favorite stores in that grand shrine to commercialism known as the mall. For this, the Eaton Centre provided him with three floors of fun. I learned it was how he spent much of his day, exploring the retail possibilities of North American culture, having happily succumbed to its evils without a fight, like the birthright of some fallen angel.

[71]

The seemingly endless supply of merchandise fascinated him. He was enchanted by how the same product could come in so many different sizes and colors, to accommodate the customer's every whim. His greatest pleasure lay in purchasing luxury items for his mother and sister, paid for with a substantial monthly subsidy from the Libyan government. What he didn't spend on food, he used to buy things for his family. Whenever one of his fellow students completed his treatment and prepared to return home, Yusuf would pack a suitcase full to bursting and send it along with them. Clothing and accessories for the adults, toys and games for a cherished nephew.

That day we trekked from store to store: Zara, Sears, American Eagle, Toys R Us. Each one contained a favorite area. Despite his flawed English and bandaged hand — or perhaps because of them — the clerks fell over themselves to help this attractive, wounded man with the beaming smile. I saw the charisma shining through the damage as he struggled to express himself, and the eagerness of the clerks to help him find the right scarf for his mother, the choicest cologne for his sister, the perfect toy for a three-year-old boy. (A talking monkey whose arms moved, as it turned out on that first outing.)

Seeing him through others' eyes, I found myself becoming more enamored of him. I had thought I would be trailing around as a sort of escort-translator, but he proved more than capable. I was pleased: here was a man who had no intention of being a victim of circumstance. He was making the most of this shiny new world and his unexpected place in it. It had been naïve of me to think it would be otherwise, especially after seeing him in a gay bar that first night.

We had a moment of whimsy in the cologne department at Sears when he sprayed a tester of Calvin Klein's *Sport* on his forearm and urged me to smell it. His face was expectant, as though he had just shared a secret pleasure with me. I sniffed it and shook my head.

"Ugh! Not for me."

He had a moment of mock indignation. "Why, Geef? Why?"

"Too flowery," I told him.

"You don't like flower?"

"Not on a man."

He breathed the scent in deeply. "This Yusuf!" he cried, spraying it all over himself.

On the escalator up to the next floor, we passed two men coming down hand-in-hand on the opposite side. Yusuf turned to me with a perplexed look.

"This gay?" he asked.

"Say it properly," I said. "Are they gay? It's plural."

"Are they gay?"

"Yes, they are gay. Just like us."

I saw him grappling with the idea. Clearly, he hadn't considered himself gay before. Understandably so. In Libya, it would be tantamount to signing one's own death warrant: *Please kill me.* He shook his head.

"Yusuf not gay," he said finally.

"No?"

He shook his head. Obviously, some cultural realignment was in order. I mentally added it to the list of educational processes I intended him to undergo so that he would be a better fit in his new hometown. A better fit for both of us.

"Well," I said, looking him up and down as though sizing him up. "Then you are a guy who likes getting blow jobs from other guys. To me, this is gay."

He smiled, but did not reply.

On our return to his room he backed me into a corner, kissing me with abandon. He pulled back and looked me over then kissed me again, long and hard, as though satisfying a hunger for something he desperately needed. The experience seemed to intoxicate him. It wasn't until later that I learned he had never kissed another man before meeting me.

Sated at last, he leaned back with a delirious expression.

"Geef, I like you!" he said breathily.

We fell on the bed, pulling off each other's clothes. This time I stopped him as he raced toward climax.

"You have to wait for me," I told him. "Understand?"

"Yes, understand," he said. "You want come."

It didn't take long. My orgasm was almost frightening in its intensity from having been delayed while I concentrated on filling his needs.

"Now Geef wash," he instructed immediately afterward.

Cleanliness, it seemed, was an obsession with him. I thought at first it was a religious thing, but of all the Muslims I met during the months we were together I never met one as fastidious as him.

I came out of the bathroom wrapped in a towel. He looked me over appraisingly and nodded.

"Is nice," he said. "Nice body."

"It's more than a body," I told him. "I also have a mind." I pointed to my head. "And a heart." I put a hand over my heart.

"I understand. Teacher have a big heart."

He smiled so dazzlingly I couldn't help feeling a little overwhelmed. I dropped the towel.

"I have other big things as well," I said, as he gazed down at my erection, still sizeable in its post-coital state. "One day Geef is going to fuck Yusuf."

He shook his head. I knew he had no intention of ever letting me dominate him sexually. For that reason alone, I was determined it would happen sooner rather than later.

"No same-same?" I asked, repeating his own expression from the other day, the implication being that what was good for one was good for the other.

He smiled at my reply, but turned away shyly without answering.

I picked up my trousers, disentangled my underwear, and slid them on. When I bent to pick up my T-shirt, I felt a cool spray hit my back as the overwhelming scent of Calvin Klein *Sport* filled the air.

"Ugh!" I cried.

He laughed as I screwed up my face then sprawled on the bed, rubbing my back against the sheets like a dog trying to scratch its behind.

"This make you think Yusuf," he told me proudly. "No one else touch Geef now."

I felt outraged by the preposterousness of his suggestion, though I was secretly flattered that he wanted to claim me for his own. It was moments like these that bonded us for what I hoped would last forever.

WANTS

The teaching was going well. I made significant progress with all my students, though none as intimately as I had with Yusuf. Both Hamid and Ibrahim finished their treatment and returned to Libya soon after. While their English had improved during my brief time with them, I wasn't convinced I'd added significantly to the storehouse of things they would need in what was sure to be for them a difficult future. In their places, I was assigned two more students with similar-sounding names. The job was already taking on the qualities of an assembly line.

Still, I could tell Marcus was pleased with my work. One day he stopped to tell me why. I had a way with these men that he hadn't seen with the other tutors. It seemed to be more of a passion with me, something personal. From time to time, I wondered if he had prised out what was going on between me and Yusuf, but if so he never gave any sign of it. Nor did Yusuf show any over-familiarity or indication of a personal bond between us while in class. That we kept well hidden, behind closed doors. So far there had been no indiscretions. It was a secret world meant only for us.

The first sour note in our relationship — for I was already calling it a relationship after just a few weeks — came the afternoon I went up to his room unexpectedly when another student failed to show up for our one-on-one tutoring session. As noted, Marcus occasionally forgot to mention when a pupil was scheduled at the hospital, leaving me with blanks in my Day-Timer. Occasionally, however, the calls came at the last moment and there was no opportunity for him to warn me. So when my pupil didn't show up for a session, I simply went upstairs and knocked on Yusuf's door.

I was expecting to find him in bed, groggy from his medication. This particular day, however, I found him poring over a website on his laptop. I assumed he was on Facebook, where he spent a good deal of his off-hours. Although Gaddafi had been overthrown and a replacement government installed, the fight for Libya was still being fought by the old-guard Muslim Brotherhood, who were the new enemy of the state. Men like Yusuf who could no longer fight on the ground were waging an ideological war online, with propaganda constantly sallying back and forth.

Yusuf let me in then headed right back to his desk and the waiting laptop. When I tried to look over his shoulder, he blocked my view. Curious, I hugged him from behind, making him squirm till I could see photos of smiling young women on the screen.

"What is this? Are you going straight on me?" I asked.

He gave me a chagrined look.

"Geef, I looking for wife."

I took another glance at the screen. He had logged into a pricey dating site.

"Why do you need a wife?" I asked, restraining an urge to point out that he already had me and that I was better for him than any wife he might find online.

"Is for immigration," he explained. "You can to help Yusuf for find wife?"

I fell silent. He glanced up in trepidation.

"Is not for worry," he said. "Geef is best for me. Girl is only for passport."

I shook my head. "You don't need a wife," I said.

"You don't need Yusuf to stay in here?"

"Yes," I said, taking his face in my hands. "I want you to stay here. With me. I love you."

I think we were both shocked by the suddenness with which I'd blurted out my feelings for him.

"It's the modern world," I explained. "Men can marry other men. I can help you get citizenship."

His expression darkened and he turned away.

"Geef, I cannot."

"Yes, you can. *We* can."

"Yusuf need to stay in here."

"Yusuf wants," I corrected. "Yusuf *wants* to stay here."

"Yusuf wants to stay here. Girl is for wife."

"You won't find anyone to do this. I can marry you. You are for me and I am for you," I told him, surprised by my vehemence and the sudden conviction that I needed to marry him. It was the only way, I told myself. Then, when we were officially together, things could begin to work out between us.

He shook his head violently.

"No, Geef. This cannot be!"

"It can," I insisted.

"Geef not understand Islam."

"I understand Islam," I said, rather naively, I now see. "Islam does not understand gay love. Love between two men or two women."

He looked away with a fearful expression. I had turned into a madman, spouting impossible, frightening things.

"In my country," he said ominously, "these take into the desert and bury in sand. Dead."

He made a brief, cutting motion with his hand as though ending something.

"This is not Libya," I pronounced slowly. "Two men can marry."

He shook his head impatiently. "Geef, please. Need to help Yusuf. What means 'preference'?"

He pointed to the screen and looked at me pleadingly.

"It means what you are looking for," I said, angered by his obstinacy. "Man, woman, whatever..."

"Yes!" he agreed. "I need woman for marry."

"You don't need a woman to marry."

Despite my knowing that problems in relationships originated when ownership and possession came into the picture, I was suddenly convinced that all he needed was me. He looked up with a pained expression: I was challenging his most basic understanding of life, telling him there was more to love than men being with women. But challenging students was what the best teachers did, I reminded myself.

"Please, Geef. Help Yusuf."

Reluctantly, I turned to the screen, running my eye down the list of questions. *Describe yourself briefly*, the instructions read. *Be sure to make yourself sound attractive to the person who is reading the ad.*

"'Are you honest?'" I read from the screen.

"What means?"

"Do you always tell the truth?"

He nodded.

"Great. Then just say, I'm a one-handed Arab faggot looking for a woman to marry for citizenship. That should do it."

Whether he fully understood my words or not, my tone of voice told him what I was thinking and feeling.

"You cannot to help Yusuf," he said, closing the laptop.

"Say it properly," I snapped. "You don't want to help Yusuf. And no, I don't want to help Yusuf find a wife!"

I was shocked to hear myself say those words, wondering where this jealous, possessive lover had come from. I, who had loved and abandoned men all over Europe, was suddenly faced with the unthinkable: I wanted this man enough to fight for him, to try to make him see things on my terms, even if he didn't understand that I was doing it for his own good.

I had often agreed to his frequent requests to write entries for him on Facebook so that his friends and family back home would know he was alive and doing well, but this I would not do.

"Yusuf," I said, turning to face him. "You will not find a woman on a website who is willing to marry you. Not if you don't love her and she doesn't love you. Do you understand?"

He pouted. "Geef not want Yusuf to stay."

"I do want you to stay," I said heatedly. "But not like this. I can't be your lover on the side if you get married to a woman. I will gladly help you get papers to claim refugee status, if that's what you want, but I will not help you fill out some fraudulent website application to try to find a wife."

I glanced down. The credit card form showed a one-time application fee of $395. Outrageous, I thought.

"Anyway, you'd be wasting your money," I said. "No one is going to reply to your ad if you say you're looking for marriage right off the bat. In the first place, you can barely speak English. In the second, any woman seriously seeking a husband is not going to marry you unless you convince her that you are in love with her and are financially secure."

He was sulking now.

"You don't like help Yusuf," he said.

"Not this way. You don't understand North American values." Would David's words ever stop haunting me? "Even if someone did respond to such an ad, she would not be appropriate for you."

"Why?"

"She would probably only be looking for sex."

"Is okay. Yusuf need to make a baby, then get passport."

I groaned in exasperation. "It doesn't work like that here," I said. "And any girl who sleeps with you after meeting you on a website would probably only be doing it for money. Do you understand?"

He shook his head, though I was sure he did in fact understand.

"No girl is going to have unprotected sex with you so you can get her pregnant. It won't happen. And if she does have unprotected sex then she is probably not clean. She will have a disease."

If nothing else, I thought I could throw the fear of poor hygiene into him — he who rushed to wash his body parts the moment we finished having sex.

He glared at me, but I did not relent. He turned down my offer to go out to eat and eventually I left him sitting there trying to figure the intricacies of on-line dating for himself.

He didn't show up for class the next day. In fact, I didn't hear from him for two more days. But I was determined not to be the first to call. On Tuesday, the day before our next private session, he called suddenly in the evening.

"Geef," he said. "I missing you. Yusuf sorry."

"I miss you too," I said, surprised by my frankness and the surge of emotions I felt on hearing his voice. "And now you understand that nothing will come of filling out an online dating site application."

My conviction was instantly deflated.

"No," he said. "Girl is coming."

"What girl? When is she coming?"

"Yesterday," he said. "Girl is coming."

I rolled my eyes. "You mean a girl came over yesterday? Past tense?"

"Yes, girl is coming from website."

I felt an unsettling combination of anger and disgust, as though I'd been betrayed by him. It made me feel uneasy to know I had been catapulted into a world of jealousy and intrigue. Such thinking was not native to me, but somehow it had become part of what I felt and believed.

"You slept with someone you met on the website?" I asked.

There was a long pause.

"Geef, I sick."

"What do you mean?"

"She is not clean, Geef. Yusuf get sick from this girl."

"I told you!" I blurted out, even as I realized how unhelpful this would be. "What happened?"

"I catch disease."

"Syphilis? Gonorrhea?"

"No, is urinary infection. I going doctor."

I almost laughed at the appropriateness of the punishment then immediately felt sorry for him.

"I'm sorry," I said. "I was mean."

"Geef, please come. I need you."

It took me all of two seconds to give in to his request.

"All right," I said. "But I won't stay."

I went over, as promised, giving him only a chaste kiss at the door, feeling as prim and proper as a virginal bride-to-be. With some coaxing he told me the details of the date, how the girl had come over and had unprotected sex with him. Then, after he fell asleep, she took $300 from his wallet and left. She was a sex worker. I wondered if she had made that clear to him before she showed up. I didn't bother to ask and, with Yusuf's rudimentary understanding of how these things worked in North America, it would never have occurred to him to ask. I did not pretend to feel sorry for him; nor did I exult in having been proved right. I simply hoped the lesson had been learned.

Still, I was not going to be won over that easily. He made it clear he hoped we would engage in sex. I kept him at a distance. Emotions aside, I didn't want to catch whatever he had. That night he went out of his way to placate me. He played some traditional Arabic music on his laptop and danced as I watched. The rhythms and sounds were wildly discordant to my Western ears, but the sensual movements of his body were sheer pleasure to my eyes.

In the midst of this, his Skype connection rang.

"Is family!" he exclaimed, racing over to the laptop.

He didn't turn down the music as I might have done, but rather he answered the call with the sound blaring. He spoke in loud, rapid Arabic to whoever was on the other end then looked at me.

"Is mother and sister," he said, keeping the screen turned from me. "Geef not look."

He turned back to the screen, still speaking loudly, then turned to me again.

"I tell them man is here, so must put cloth." He patted his head to indicate the headscarves worn by women.

After another moment, he said to me, "Okay, Geef. I tell them you are English tutor."

I was surprised to see his mother, a young-looking woman, as well as his sister and his grandmother crowded around the screen. All three had donned head scarves. On hearing of my presence, Yusuf explained, his brother, Omar, had left the room. He did not want to meet the foreigner teaching Yusuf English. To this young Muslim man, non-Muslims were seen as evil incarnate, living a decadent Western lifestyle associated with alcohol, homosexuality, and non-submissive women. If I had spoken Arabic, I would happily have told him he was right on all counts.

We had a stilted conversation as Yusuf introduced us. His mother and grandmother spoke no English, though his sister, Yasmin, was surprisingly proficient. After a brief introduction, I nodded my pleasantries then left Yusuf to speak with them alone.

As I stepped aside, his mother began haranguing him in Arabic. It went on for a while. She sounded harsh and angry. Nevertheless, Yusuf seemed to be agreeing with what she said. After he ended the call, I asked what she had been upset about.

"She tell me, 'Yusuf wasting time. You need to wife.'"

"She said you need a wife?"

"She say Yusuf need stay here. Not coming back to Libya or die. Many bombs. Boom-boom. Need to wife."

He nearly fell over laughing. I, on the other hand, did not find it so amusing. For the first time, I became aware of the pressures he was facing from his family on top of everything else he had to deal with in his life.

Afterwards, as I made leaving noises, Yusuf pleaded with me to stay with him that night. I resisted half-heartedly, but eventually gave in to his request. For the first time since I began staying over, we did not have sex. We fell asleep in each other's arms.

CARS

I never really got a handle on all the medication Yusuf was taking, both for his physical needs as much as his mental and emotional well-being, but I was beginning to be aware of the mood swings they caused, as well as the obvious — and sometimes not-so-obvious — repercussions. One day he woke and, without so much as a "good morning", asked me to help him buy a car online. My mind did somersaults trying to imagine him navigating the streets with just one hand.

"This is nuts," I said. "You won't be able to drive here. Do you even have a driver's license?"

"Need to help Yusuf," he pouted, his eyes pleading with that look I was by now oh-so-familiar with.

"I *don't* need to help Yusuf," I snapped back.

Since arriving, he had come to view the Internet as an endless bazaar, a place for finding anything from automobiles to wives. And, without realizing it, I had become his secretary and manservant, designated to accommodate his every whim.

"Geef, I not ask you to pay," he explained patiently, as though that were the reason for my refusal. "Yusuf have money."

"Bloody good thing," I said, knowing that with my finances I couldn't have paid even if I'd wanted to. And I wouldn't have wanted to in a million years.

Calmly and slowly, he explained his reasoning: cars were far cheaper in North America than anything he could purchase overseas. He wanted me to help him find something second-hand to ship back to Libya. A red light snapped on in my mind. This meant he was still thinking of returning home one day. He went to his laptop and called up a number of online sites with used cars for sale, pointing out the prices and models he was interested in.

I didn't like where this was heading.

"It's dangerous to buy things on the Internet," I objected. Things like wives, I was thinking, but refrained from saying so. "People get scammed and lose their money."

"Is not scam. Is good price."

His faith in the Internet was so naïve it galled me.

"This is nonsense," I said. "You should be concerned with getting better, not buying all this junk. Your health is the important thing to concentrate on right now."

"Geef, I am do everything for health."

He put his hand on his heart. The gesture was beginning to annoy me.

"It's not a good idea," I told him.

He shrugged. "Okay, you not need to help Yusuf. I will do."

Lately, the news from Libya had not been reassuring. The country seemed to be unravelling politically. I kept telling him that returning home might become an impossibility and that he needed to save his money in case that happened. Word on the street was that outside interests were purposely keeping the government unstable long enough to gain control of the oil fields. An American ambassador and his wife had recently been killed in Benghazi, and the country was on the verge of civil war again. But he was having none of my reasoning.

"Why don't you wait?" I asked, exasperated. "If you send it over now it will just sit there and rot. Keep your money."

"No, Geef. Brother Yusuf like to drive."

"Great," I said. "Your brother Omar, who hates you for turning against Islam by learning English, is going to benefit from this transaction. Why even bother?"

It was only later that I realized this was a way for him to stay connected with his family, along with all the other gifts he sent back home. It was also his way of showing off. To me they seemed empty gestures: Look what Yusuf can do from across the world, he seemed to be saying. But to him they mattered greatly.

He gave me his hurt look, the one that was supposed to win arguments when his words could not.

"Family is most important," he told me solemnly.

"Really?" I asked, thinking of my own relations. I couldn't have agreed less at that moment, but I wasn't willing to delve into my personal history to prove a point that would be lost on him.

"Cannot you to helping Yusuf?" he asked.

I rolled my eyes. "Say it correctly. Can you help Yusuf?"

"Yes!" he said, smiling and knowing he had won me over again.

He jumped into my arms and wrapped his legs around my waist, forcing me to carry him over to the bed where we soon became a tangle of limbs.

INDOCTRINATION

My patience was being sorely tested by Yusuf's fascination for First World luxuries. As David had warned me, outsiders saw us as a Land of Plenty and, for the most part, they are right. We have all the useless junk that money can buy.

Once again I recalled David's injunction that Yusuf's mentality might not allow him to adapt to North American traditions. His adherence to religious strictures was obviously a sign of that. But could he change? Despite indications to the contrary, I was determined he would. All of this fueled my intention to get his thinking on the right path, one that would save him from himself. It never occurred to me that he might need saving from me as well.

Apart from David, I had few friends in the city. There were, however, people I ran into from time to time, regulars in the neighborhood. A small number of these might, I hoped, offer opportunities for socializing. The influence of others, I reasoned, would give Yusuf a broader range of human interaction and rub off on him in a positive way.

As far as I was concerned, Yusuf had lived much of his life in darkness. I felt I could make him see the light so long as I kept pointing it out to him. I knew, for instance, that he would need a job once his rehabilitation was complete. If he were rootless, it would be a disaster for us both no matter how good our intentions. I'd already made a few inquiries to learn what his school credits were worth in today's workforce. It looked bleak. Most of what he had learned would not be given equivalent technical accreditation in Canada. He would need to repeat a good deal of what he'd already studied to work in the medical profession. I wasn't sure he had the patience or the mental acumen for it in his current state.

In addition, his English wasn't yet good enough to attempt a full-time study program. All the while, however, I kept telling myself he would make a good partner if I could deprogram him from his upbringing. I'd convinced myself it was something I was doing for him rather than an act borne of my selfish desires. When the time came, I was even prepared to marry him if we both felt it was the right thing to do. Wasn't that in itself proof of my good intentions?

Before leaving the city, Jerod had introduced me to what he called his "quality neighbors." They were a straight couple living down the hall. I kept running into them in the lobby and the elevator, so when they invited me to dinner the following Friday I asked if I could bring Yusuf along as my date. I explained that his English was minimal and hoped it wouldn't be a problem. Bravely, they declared they were more than happy to include him.

My desire to bring him to the party was triggered in part by an incident outside the hotel a few days prior to that. We had been navigating a busy intersection on Yonge Street when a woman with a small terrier headed directly across our path. I thought nothing of it when the dog pulled away from its owner and sniffed curiously at Yusuf's leg. Yusuf froze. Then, without warning, he kicked the dog. It yelped — more in fear than pain, I suspect — but its owner was furious. How dare he attack her dog? She threatened to have him arrested for cruelty to animals.

Before I could deescalate the situation, the lights turned from green to yellow then red. Suddenly, we were stranded in the middle of the intersection with cars surging all around us. The woman's tirade continued. She wasn't backing down. I calmed the situation as best I could, making up excuses as I went along, explaining that Yusuf had thought her dog was going to bite him. I made him show her his damaged hand. He was genuinely afraid, I argued. Yet I knew it wasn't fear that had made him do it. Rather, it was an ingrained belief in Islamic culture that dogs are unclean. He had already said as much to me on several occasions.

Horns were honking. Drivers rolled their windows down to yell at the three lunatics and a dog blocking traffic in the middle of the intersection. Undaunted, I made Yusuf lean down and pet the animal, despite the fact that each seemed equally terrified of the other at that moment. At first he protested, but when I insisted he finally gave in. The dog adapted quicker, being the more diplomatic of the two, and licked Yusuf's hand as though to acknowledge his wound. How many times did I wish later that it could have done the same to his heart and mind?

The lights changed again and we parted, Yusuf and I going on to the hotel, the woman and her dog heading wherever they were going before our paths crossed. I held my tongue as we walked. I didn't want to belittle him for his behavior on top of everything else, but it served yet again to point up the vast cultural divide between us.

Strangely, the encounter seemed to inspire a manic episode with him. He talked about the dog all the way up the elevator and down the hallway to his room, making it sound as though he had just made an important new friend. I became more determined than ever to acclimatize — or indoctrinate him — as quickly as I could.

Friday came. Yusuf was extremely nervous about going to his first Canadian party. He spent an inordinate amount of time before the mirror in the bathroom, fussing with his hair and clothes, but at last he emerged and declared himself ready. I saw that he was dressed all wrong. He had on a loud orange sweatshirt and loose-fitting jeans. On his feet he wore a pair of fluorescent green sneakers. He looked like a teenage hip-hop star rather than a mature adult going to a cocktail party.

"Is all right?" he asked.

"I guess," I replied, not knowing whether to knock his confidence or boost it.

"Wait!" he cried, and ran back into the bathroom, emerging with his Calvin Klein *Sport*.

"No!" I cried, wresting it from him, knowing his tendency to overdose on cologne. "You do not wear this to parties."

"But, Geef? Why?"

"Because people don't like it. People are allergic to scents."

He pouted. "Crazy people," he said, but gave in to my demands.

When we got to the neighbours' door, we heard music and loud conversations from inside. I raised my hand to knock.

"Wait, Geef," Yusuf said. I turned to him. He shook his head forlornly, looking as though he might bolt. "I cannot."

"You'll be fine," I said, and gave him my best smile.

My knock fell heavily on the door. Before he could say more, the door opened and a petite blonde stood there. It was Sally, one of our hosts.

"Geoffrey!" she shrieked, clearly high or drunk or both.

She hugged me then reached out for Yusuf, who tentatively extended his uninjured hand and let her hold it for a moment. Sally welcomed him with a kiss on the cheek.

"He's gorgeous! He looks like Omar Sharif!" she gushed, disregarding his outfit entirely.

A smile lit up Yusuf's face. He did, indeed, resemble a ghetto version of the film star.

We followed Sally in. The apartment was wall-to-wall people, an overwhelming prospect for anyone uninitiated with such events. I said hello to everyone I knew by sight, introducing Yusuf as my partner, which is how I had come to think of him by then. The other guests made all the appropriate responses. A few of them took note of his wardrobe. Some looked amused by it, but no one said anything untoward.

At first Yusuf clung to me, fearful of venturing from my side. When he had begun to feel a bit more secure, he wandered off on his own. I kept an eye on him, but for the most part he seemed to be faring well, making small talk with whoever approached for a closer look at this exotic specimen.

The room held a good mix of academics, hipsters and political types, including a lesbian Muslim journalist known for her outspokenness. I kept trying to steer Yusuf in her direction, hoping she might help shed some light on how social views on sexuality were changing, though we never made it over to her corner for a chat. I was disappointed when she left before Yusuf could talk to her.

I watched as he made his way around the room, at first shyly then openly and even enthusiastically as he slowly found himself accepted. People seemed to regard him with friendly curiosity. I saw a few smile and shake their heads at what he was saying. No doubt their comprehension suffered with the flurry of speech he generated when he got excited and the words got ahead of him.

Funnier still was his drinking, a habit he had quickly taken to despite his cultural prohibitions. Unaccustomed to alcohol, it took only one drink to get him drunk. Two could send him over the edge. I watched him begin his second beer then snatched it out of his hand before he could finish it.

A sheepish smile lit up his face. "Geef watching me," he said. "Like father trying to control me."

"Yes," I told him. "Somebody's got to."

We stayed for almost two hours then said our goodbyes. He staggered frequently on the way back to the hotel, his face lit up with a smile. At one point I stopped him from walking into a lamppost and later grabbed his arm to keep him from crossing the road without looking first. At times like these he was clearly a danger to himself. I worried I wouldn't always be there to watch out for him.

Despite my prodding him with questions about the party, he was mostly silent as we walked. It was as if he needed time to digest what he had heard and seen during the course of the evening. I knew not to worry, however. When anything angered or upset him it came out right away. On the other hand, if it was a matter of unraveling the thoughts in his head, it could take a while before comprehension dawned.

Outside the hotel he stopped and turned to me, putting his good hand on my shoulder.

"Geef, is such a big thing here. I am shaking."

He shook his head. Clearly, something had overwhelmed him.

"What do you mean?"

He laughed happily. "Here is black, white and other. Man, woman. Narrow and fat. Everything is coming to Canadian party!"

The arrow had hit home. It was my sly indoctrination of an "Everybody is equal!" philosophy. I felt like a John Lennon and Yoko Ono campaigner: Love, Peace and War is Over if You Want it. I had hoped it marked the beginning of our successful transition as a couple.

COMMUNITY

Before leaving for Europe, I had carried on a casual friendship with a gay man from Yemen who lived in Toronto. Arraf was a writer. We met through mutual friends. We didn't stay in touch when I left, but one day while walking through the village not long after my return I ran into him again. It seemed serendipitous. He had recently published his memoirs about being a gay Muslim — to great acclaim from the liberal sector, but also to scathing, hate-filled responses from fellow Islamists, in Canada and abroad, who vilified him openly and threatened his life online. Not one to pass up an opportunity, he'd used the threats to bolster his claim for refugee status with this irrefutable proof that his life was in danger should he be forced to return to Yemen.

We exchanged numbers. I called him a few weeks later. Arraf's schedule was light in those days, so I asked him to indulge me on a personal matter. We went for coffee in the village to catch up. Before I knew it, I was spilling my guts about Yusuf — how I loved him, how I wanted to marry him to make it possible for him to remain in Toronto after his surgery. We sat and talked for more than an hour. He told me of his own struggles to free himself from the strictures of his previous life, of having to hide his sexuality in Yemen and of the fear for his life — not in the least exaggerated, he said — all the while assuring me that what I wanted for Yusuf was possible, but only if Yusuf was one-hundred percent sure he wanted it too.

"It has to be his choice," he warned me. "Otherwise, it won't work. He has to want to be here and accept First World ways and everything that entails."

He echoed what David had already said in different ways. I agreed with him, but admitted I wasn't sure if Yusuf truly wanted for himself what I hoped for him. I described Yusuf's efforts to secure a wife and the minor misfortune it had led to. Arraf laughed. It had started to seem funny to me in hindsight, too, though the incident still stung. Then I mentioned that Yusuf prayed five times a day.

Arraf gave me a hesitant look.

"He's knows he's gay, but still clings to his old habits?"

I nodded.

He shook his head. "Maybe I should have a talk with him and give him a slap on the head. Doesn't he understand he's in the New World and should take advantage of the freedoms here?"

"That's what he's struggling with," I said.

"It's not something everyone grows out of," he said, again echoing David's sentiment about the need to change his thinking. "How old is he?"

"Twenty-five."

"Then there's hope."

He told me about an immigration specialist at a downtown community center, explaining how she had helped many gay and lesbian Muslims make a safe transition while escaping from homophobic countries around the world. He wrote her name on a napkin and handed it to me.

"Take your boy to see her," he concluded. "She can point him in the right direction."

"Thanks for all your help," I said. "It's been great seeing you again."

He stood and nodded. "Good to see you again too. I just hope you know what you're getting into."

I was excited to know there was a potential network in place to help people like Yusuf. I phoned immediately to tell him the good news. I heard the hesitation in his voice.

"Geef, this man you speak — he is Muslim?"

"Yes," I said. "He's already gone through the process. He can help guide you through it."

"Is not good," he told me darkly.

"Why?" I asked, disheartened by his response.

"This is Muslim in small community. He friend with other Muslims. He telling people Yusuf gay."

"No, it's not like that!" I exclaimed. "I explained your situation to him. He knows the danger you're in. He understands what it takes to emigrate here to live a safe life where you can be free from worry about such things."

The argument spun round in circles, as so many things with Yusuf did, fear being the constant trigger in discussions of anything to do with his personal life.

"I have the name of someone at the community center. Will you at least come with me and talk to her?"

"Geef, I don't like."

"She can speak to you anonymously," I said. "We don't have to tell her your real name."

I had failed to convince him by the time the conversation was over. Still, I was determined to set up a meeting with the counselor. If Yusuf didn't want to come with me then I would go alone. That way at least one of us would know what the procedure entailed when it came time to follow through on it.

Getting an appointment was relatively easy. Working on Yusuf to join me took a bit longer. In fact, it was another two weeks of badgering before he relented. On the day in question we walked to the centre together with Yusuf arguing all the way while I tried to bolster his confidence. By the time we got there, he'd worked himself into a fit of nerves. He begged me to turn around and cancel the appointment, spouting every reason he could think of as proof that it was wrong for him: he was a good Muslim; it was just coming up to Ramadan; he wasn't really gay; someone would find out he'd been there and tell his fellow Muslims, leading to who-knew-what unspeakable disaster.

He was terrified of talking to anyone about his predicament. I recognized this by then, but I didn't accept it as a valid reason not to try. As we entered the lobby, Yusuf's hands were shaking. I walked over to reception and gave our first names. The young man at the desk smiled and asked us to take a seat.

Twenty minutes went by. Yusuf's growing nervousness and my exasperation with his reluctance felt almost tangible, like opposing forces on a collision course. When I returned to the desk to enquire about the delay, the receptionist apologized and assured me that we would be seen soon.

I went back to explain this to Yusuf, but he shook his head and stood.

"Geef, I cannot stay!"

"It's just a talk," I said. "What are you so worried about?"

"Geef, I worried for my life."

He glanced out the window to the street, as though expecting to see an assassin aiming a gun at him.

"Please," I said. "Do this for me. This is so we can end this, so you won't have to live in fear for the rest of your life. Please trust me!"

Just then a soft-spoken black woman came down the broad staircase to meet us. She introduced herself as Karla and invited us up to her office. I fell in line behind her and we climbed the stairs together, Yusuf trailing silently behind me, as though he were going to his own execution.

In Karla's office, Yusuf sat looking down at the floor. He was unable or unwilling to speak for himself. I briefly explained his case. Karla nodded. Becoming a refugee claimant on grounds of sexual orientation was a possibility, she explained. If accepted, it meant that Yusuf could get a work permit. At this point he found his voice.

"I won't be cleaner," he said, looking up as his pride asserted itself. "I am medical student."

Suddenly, it was as if all his fears had boiled down to this one very practical concern.

"Well, then you would have to have a means of support," Karla said patiently.

"I will support him," I said, thinking in a panic of my meager funds and less than optimal work history.

"Then that leads us to option number two," Karla continued, directing her statements to Yusuf. "You can marry a Canadian citizen — it can be a man or a woman. But if you do that, you won't be given permission to work immediately. So then either you would have to have another source of income or your spouse" — here she looked at me — "would have to support you."

"I am not marry to man. This I cannot do," Yusuf said firmly, looking directly at her for the first time. "I have pension from Libya government."

Karla looked at him with something like pity. "They would cut it off the minute you apply for refugee status."

Yusuf looked crushed. He hadn't considered the possibility. Perhaps he was just beginning to understand how trapped he really was. It's a fear all refugee claimants must face at some point or another.

"If you're interested," she told him in a gentle voice, "there is a private group for gay Muslims who worship and keep their faith together. I can put you in touch with them. You would be able to discuss the situation with others who are going through what you are going through."

The fearful look returned to Yusuf's eyes.

"Gay Muslims?" he repeated. "This true?"

He seemed more alarmed than hopeful at the news, scarcely able to believe that there could be others in his situation.

Karla nodded. "Yes, quite a number of them. They meet at a private residence, so they cannot be disturbed or picketed by hostile forces. It's completely safe. I can give you a contact number."

She wrote a name and number on a slip of paper and handed it to Yusuf. He stared at it guardedly for a moment before picking it up and putting it in his pocket.

There was little left to say. Karla urged Yusuf to think about the things she had told him. And, if he had additional questions, she would be happy to answer them or refer him to someone else if she could not. I thanked her for her time and for informing us of the options and the hurdles facing us.

We left.

Out on the street, Yusuf found his voice again. He spoke agitatedly: what I was suggesting was not possible. It would be far too difficult, at least according to the thumbnail sketch Karla had provided.

"It's not difficult," I said, stopping his rant. "It's complicated, but it's not difficult. And I will help you through every step."

He gave me a stony stare. "What is difference?"

I tried to explain how something could be complicated but not difficult.

He looked at me and said, "You are complicated. Especially when you talk."

I stopped to consider this, "Yes, I am complicated, but I am not difficult. You, on the other hand are not complicated at all, but you are very, very difficult."

He laughed a little. It was the best reaction I would get from him till he calmed down again.

On the way back, we stopped at his favourite halal grocery to buy some cuts of lamb. Yusuf sounded almost cheerful as he described a soup he would make for me that evening.

"Celebration, Geef. Yusuf cook for you!"

I wasn't sure what it was we were celebrating. The day had felt mostly like a failure to me.

In the supermarket, a large television screen blared overhead. CNN was covering a bombing in Damascus. War in the Middle East had not only continued, but had proliferated since the Arab Spring. The bombings still shocked the world, while Syria went undefended, resulting in hundreds of thousands, if not millions, of displaced refugees. I feared the outflow had just begun. Meanwhile, Western leaders discussed more efficient ways of targeting their foes, resulting in fewer casualties for their side.

Go ahead and kill them, I thought. But you won't solve the problem. You will simply defer them to the next generation. Education is the only hope. Otherwise one dead martyr will just give rise to another and another, till someday they will rise up and kill us all.

WAR

I had told David what little I knew of Yusuf's background, but there was so much more I didn't know. I used to believe that a person's life experiences did not necessarily add up to the whole person. I believed that who we are intrinsically — the person we are inside — is ultimately what counts, and anything that doesn't fit the picture will wash off like water from a duck's back. I was wrong, of course. Like Heraclitus, I believed character was destiny. But Heraclitus hedged his bets by adding that there is nothing permanent in this world except change. We all change.

Yusuf came from a country of far greater changes than anything I had experienced in my lifetime, and perhaps none greater than the one that began on the fifteenth of February, 2011, in his hometown of Benghazi. It was his twenty-second birthday. That morning, along with messages from well-wishers, he received an email urging him to join a gathering at police headquarters to protest the arrest of activist Fathi Terbil. Terbil was a lawyer who represented the families of a number of prisoners murdered by Gaddafi's security forces in prison. Terbil had enjoyed support from many freedom-loving Libyans, who saw his arrest as a slap in the face of human rights.

Yusuf was late getting to the protest. Luckily so, as it turned out. He arrived just in time to see the army fire on the protestors. Hundreds were killed and many wounded, including some of his friends and fellow students. He was fortunate to escape serious injury himself.

The event would prove a turning point in the country's tumultuous history. Inspired by recent uprisings in Egypt and Saudi Arabia, as well as by the so-called Arab Spring in nearby Tunisia, political activists sent up a cry over the Internet, calling for struggle and solidarity. The dogs of war had been loosed.

With the protests came an official "Day of Rage" as the revolt spread. Yusuf was already a medical student at the time. Practicing on cadavers had been as close as he'd come to death till then. He was about to see and feel it up close.

Libya has been called a kleptocracy. I appreciated the word, with its combination of the Greek *kleptes*, or thief, and *kratos*, power or rule. Rule by thieves. It's a form of corruption where the government exists largely to accumulate and protect the wealth of its leaders at the expense of its citizens.

That was what Libya had become since its leader, Colonel Muammar Gaddafi, took power in a coup in 1969, single-handedly ruling the country for more than forty years. Predictably, Gaddafi clamped down on the protests, claiming that the protesters were trying to subvert government forces. It's a rhetoric that has been repeated throughout history, every time someone demands justice. The fact is, there can be no non-violent revolutions.

Yusuf's participation in the war was motivated by his medical training. When his classes were halted, he took charge of a lumbering ambulance that followed the fighting on the outskirts of Benghazi, hauling the wounded back to hospitals when he could, or, when he could not, treating them in the field until they either recovered or died.

By and large, the rebel fighters were ordinary civilians: students, teachers, and oil workers. Later, they were joined by disgruntled police officers and army defectors who helped form a people's army.

The West had grown used to thinking of the Middle East as a more or less unified geographical entity, one that shared ethnic and cultural affiliations characterized by what some saw as a backward-facing theology. What we couldn't see was the fierce suppression of a strong desire to evolve and join the modern world — a desire that was shared by a great many people, especially the young.

As I pointed out to David, change had been opposed by the country's leaders for so long that it was a matter of when it would happen, not if. The old guard wanted things to stay as they were, while the young wanted to modernize. Conflict was inevitable. It's the way of the world. Conservative factions will always clash with those who want fewer personal restraints and more liberalization. Still, it didn't explain the polarities and divisions that already existed within the Arab world itself, the constant friction between rival factions. In fact, apart from a shared linguistic background there was little real unity between Arab nations, and it was beginning to tear the Middle East apart.

Gaddafi grew increasingly desperate as unrest took hold of the country. At first, he blamed the rebellion on Al-Qaeda and Osama bin Laden, even suggesting that the Western demons of alcohol and illegal drugs were affecting the minds of the rebels. He went further, claiming that Europe and America were at the heart of the unrest. None of these accusations helped restore the balance of power, however. Proclaiming himself a warrior for the people, Gaddafi stated he would die a martyr rather than give in to rebel demands. His prophecy was about to come true.

As the revolt spread, Gaddafi tried unsuccessfully to shut down the Internet. Had he done so earlier, he might have quelled the fighting. The Libyan Civil War became the first rebellion conducted online, a true people's revolution, as one by one Gaddafi's international allies dropped their support of his government and his followers resigned or left in disgrace.

The fighting continued throughout that spring and into summer. As I related to David, Yusuf was there when the rebel forces broke into one of Gaddafi's luxury palaces, a fortified bunker designed to withstand a nuclear attack. Of all the reports of atrocities, both confirmed and unconfirmed, there is one I know to be true. I know it because Yusuf showed me the photos he took of a twelve-year-old servant girl, her face and body covered in blisters from boiling water thrown on her by Gaddafi's bodyguards as they abandoned the palace. What her crime was, I never learned. Most likely she was a victim of the rage and fear incited in the guards by the oncoming forces of liberation. Yusuf said the girl screamed as the rebels stormed the palace, believing her torturers had returned to kill her. He calmed her down, sedated her, and brought her to the hospital for treatment, just one of thousands of victims of the barbarities perpetrated by fighters on both sides.

Gaddafi himself was captured and killed by rebel forces in Sirte, his hometown, some weeks later. There are varying reports of his death, none of them pleasant. According to eye-witnesses, he was impaled on a stake shoved anally through his body, a traditional queer's death. In fact, some claimed Gaddafi was a secret queer — a crime punishable by death under Islam.

Yusuf showed me online pictures of the palace, a luxury stronghold with swimming pools, a private amusement park, and a small zoo stocked with nine lions. The rebel forces discovered such items as gold-plated guns and a couch made of solid gold in the shape of a reclining mermaid whose face was modelled after one of Gaddafi's daughters. A poster of actor Jake Gyllenhall in his role as the sweaty, bare-chested Prince of Persia hung on a wall in his office. A gay pornographic tape was found in the colonel's private desk. Bizarre but, apparently, true.

Nowadays this is all fodder for the curious to gape at and wonder about from a safe and comfortable distance. But what did it mean for the thousands, like Yusuf, who lived the reality — those who were forced to confront it firsthand? I still can't say. But what I now know and can say with certainty is this: such experiences stay with us forever. They form us and shape us. They do not slide off like water from a duck's back.

PRIDE

WorldPride was fast approaching, marking the forty-fifth anniversary of the Stonewall Riots. Whenever I mentioned it, however, Yusuf insisted he wasn't interested in seeing or participating in it in any way. I was determined that he would.

It was a case of the immovable object meeting the irresistible force, which pretty much summed up our relationship at the time. In any case, I knew resistance was futile. His hotel stood a mere block from where the parade was to make its final turn off Yonge Street before heading to eventual dissolution.

I see now that once Yusuf witnessed the event the sheer magnitude of it stunned him. It broke down some inner resistance, after which he saw the world from a different standpoint, one not conditioned by twenty-five years in a repressive society. I think he began to comprehend that people really could sustain a lifestyle of their choosing. that men could love and live openly with other men. But that still didn't remove the constant pressure put on him by a mother who berated him during every conversation about the need to marry a woman, or a brother who shunned him for learning English and fraternizing with non-Muslims. I had yet to encounter his father, but I thought I could imagine how he felt. Only Yusuf's sister, Yasmin, seemed to have any sense of her brother's changed circumstances. To her the New World represented freedom, not a weakening and corrupting of the spirit. I was glad when I heard her encourage him to stay in Canada during one of their frequent Skype sessions. She seemed to have taken a liking to me, regarding me as a positive influence on Yusuf.

Pride Sunday rolled around. The growing crowds passing through the hotel lobby piqued Yusuf's curiosity. After considerable effort on my part and much grumbling on Yusuf's, I convinced him to come out and watch the parade with me. We slipped through an opening in the barricades and made our way across the street. The sidewalks thronged with people. I watched Yusuf glance nervously around to see who might recognize him amidst the masses of people. I tried to reason with him by saying that the likelihood of seeing someone he knew was low. Even so, anyone who saw him there could likewise be seen by him.

"Turn it around," I suggested. "If anyone questions why you are here, you can do the same in return."

This seemed to reassure him. He relaxed as he began to pick out some of the outrageous costumes. It wasn't long before a pounding beat announced the arrival of the floats; soon we were focused on the colorful pageantry passing before us. With two hundred and eighty organizations, and more than twelve thousand people registered to march, the parade was estimated at five hours. It would be the longest Pride I'd ever experienced.

For a while, all went well. Yusuf dropped his self-consciousness and began to enjoy the ostentation as I pointed out the various organizations, including health-care workers, the firefighter's association, and even the police. We were surrounded by parents with small children hoisted onto their shoulders. But for the sultry summer heat, we might have been watching a Santa Claus parade. Clearly, it was nothing like what he'd anticipated and feared.

As we stood there, however, I suddenly saw his face darken. I looked up at a float passing directly in front of us. Balloons strained skywards. A banner read: *Rainbow Coalition*. On board the truck, two topless women coated in body paint and glitter sprayed the crowd with water guns.

Yusuf turned to me with an outraged expression.

"Geef, why you bring me here? This terrible!"

I'd long been accustomed to seeing topless women in the parade and never considered that it might be a shock for him.

"This is what Pride is for," I said, trying to downplay it. "It's about freedom and the right to be ourselves."

He muttered something in Arabic then turned angrily and stalked off, pushing his way through the crowd. I followed, fearful of what he might do. At the corner, he stopped abruptly. The barricades blocked his way. There was no way of getting past the floats and marchers, back to the safety of the hotel.

As he stood there, a drag queen in a feather dress and frizzy pink wig planted herself directly in front of him. Yusuf shrank from her as she reached out and touched his hair, shaking her oversized bosoms in his face. He tensed. For an instant, I thought he might attack her in his confusion and anger.

A few feet away, two policemen watched them with amusement. When Yusuf saw them laughing it seemed to confuse him even more. Here were symbols of authority, witnessing the mayhem and yet tolerating it benignly. To his way of thinking, it must have seemed sheer madness — the world had gone completely awry.

Then suddenly, unexpectedly, he laughed. I watched as he turned to look over his shoulder, his eyes searching me out in the crowd. I waved to let him know I was still within reach. He beckoned me onward. As I reached him, he handed me his cell phone.

"Geef, take a picture."

He draped an arm over the shoulder of the drag queen posing for her moment of glory. Suddenly, for Yusuf, it was nothing more than a gigantic party extending up and down the length of the street. Looking back, I doubt I could ever have put myself in his situation and comprehended what he was experiencing at that moment. The absolute freedom, the concept of a life without restrictions, must have blown his mind.

I took his hand. For the next hour we stood there, side by side, watching the parade, just one more carefree couple joining the ranks of thousands of partiers. Something happened to him that day, but whether it was ultimately for good or for bad I can't say.

We all come to these junctures in life when we realize we're standing on the edge of a cliff. Reason tells us we have two choices: the first is to take a leap of faith; the second is to back off and forever lose the moment when actual change might have come had we had the courage to accept it. There is no third choice. But having once stood on that cliff edge one thing is certain — we can never return to being who we were before.

In the days and weeks that followed, Yusuf turned to me more than once to proclaim his amazement at how I'd changed his life. He said it so often I began to wonder if there was a hidden message in those pronouncements, some play on words he was getting at. Each time, I would ask him if he thought it was for the better.

"Yes," he said. "Always better with Geef. When I with Geef, I am happy."

I should have stopped there and let him contemplate the abyss, at least until he grew comfortable with it. For I see now that, despite the amazement he felt at this revelation, he still had not fully made the choice to accept it. In the meantime, I decided to push forward while I had the advantage. I explained that he shouldn't let tradition dictate his life and that he needn't worry what his mother and father might expect of him while he lived halfway across the world. It was easy enough for me, with all my experience, to advise him, but a part of him still clung to the old ways of thinking. The arguments were circular: he did those things because they were right. If I asked what made them right, he would say it was because that was the way things were done in his country. If I reminded him that he was no longer in Libya, he would simply shake his head. As time went on, however, his arguments grew less vehement, his convictions less strong. It seemed to me he only wanted convincing that what he was doing was right. And foolishly, I believed I had convinced him.

That night, after the parade, we went through the dozens of pictures I had snapped of him that day. Looking them over, Yusuf shook his head but his expression was happy.

"This Pride?" he asked, glancing up from his laptop like some kid thrilled that an older, much-admired brother had just given him his first forbidden sip of alcohol.

"Yes, this is Pride."

He nodded. "Crazy Pride."

NIGHTMARES

I haven't mentioned Yusuf's nightmares. Anyone who suffers from post-traumatic stress can tell you they are the bane of your existence. With drugs and professional help, you can keep the terrors at bay in the daytime to a degree, but whatever trauma lies buried deep in your psyche will emerge and turn your world completely around while you are defenseless in sleep.

For Yusuf, the nightmares were a constant problem the entire time we were together, except for the occasional night when all was calm in his world or when his medication got upped to the point where there was little difference between sleeping and being comatose. At those times, when he was excessively medicated, he exhibited what I called his alternate personality. He would become edgy and obsessive, but at the same time eerily vacant, as if he had forgotten who or where he was. His eyes glittered wildly and he would stop answering my questions. It was then I most clearly understood that I was dealing with someone whose very existence lay far from all that was ordinary and predictable in my world.

I give him all due credit: he seldom feared anything in the waking world, apart from the prospect of a future lived openly with me, of course. When you come face to face with mortality, as he had, there is little about everyday life that can scare you.

But the nightmares that haunted his sleep were a never ending torment that often propelled him bolt upright in bed, gasping for breath and clutching at some invisible enemy, as if he was being smothered by unseen hands.

Sometimes I found it hard to distinguish between the terrors in his head and the ones that appeared on the horizons of his waking world. He never forgot his life back home in Libya, where his mother, father, sister, and brother lived. If he could, I know Yusuf would have brought them all over to live with him. As it was, he lived a second existence on Skype at night, talking to them about their daily lives, trying to stay informed about what they were doing and everything that was happening back in the country he had helped liberate.

His father, who was seldom at home, worked in the oil fields for a German company, while his mother kept house. His brother, Omar, was in the military and his sister, Yasmin, was studying to be a dentist.

"This my family," he said, when he first told me about them. "We are simple family."

It was such a plain, heartfelt statement. This is who I am, he seemed to be saying. He never tired of updating me on his conversations with them, even the brother, who was so opposed to his life in Canada.

I have no doubt he loved them all and, for that, they were a source of constant worry. One day while out on patrol, his brother was shot in the leg and taken to hospital following a clash with militants. Yusuf spoke about the incident for weeks, long after his brother had left the hospital and was out of danger. The irony was that the country's current rebels had been the forces in power under Gaddafi, while Yusuf and the others had been the rebels of his day. From military to rebel, from rebel to Freedom Fighter. And so the forces of destiny toss us about as they will.

Another time, his mother called to report that a car bomb had blown up directly across the street from Yusuf's house. The city of Benghazi and its people were constantly under siege. Yusuf was agonizingly aware of this; it left him feeling agitated and longing to get back to continue the fight.

One night while I was at my apartment getting ready for bed, the phone rang. I glanced at the clock. It was nearly midnight. I knew it could only be Yusuf. I thought perhaps he was calling to wish me goodnight or to report on a conversation he'd had with his family.

His voice sounded awful: "Geef, somebody dead. Come — I need you."

Without questioning his need, I quickly dressed then headed to the hotel, treading down the long, carpeted hallway with alarm. When he didn't answer my knock, I let myself in with a duplicate pass card, which I now carried at all times. The lights were on, but the room was empty. The curtains had been pulled back and were blowing inward. I had a moment of panic before I found him on the balcony, staring out at the night sky. His eyes had that vacant look I'd seen before, a soulless expression which made him seem to have receded far from the present, slipping away to some inner realm where he could be alone with his suffering.

"Yusuf?" I called softly.

No answer.

"Yusuf!"

After a moment he looked over, as though my arrival had just registered with him.

"Talk to me," I said. "What's happening?"

He turned a mournful gaze on me.

"Geef, tonight I have no words."

"Speak. Say what cannot be said."

"Tonight, nice boy is dead."

I tried to take this in, to comprehend what he was saying.

"Someone back home?"

He nodded slowly.

"A friend has died?"

"Yes," he replied at last. "Friend from Benghazi. Bad men kill him."

His responses were painfully slow, the words hesitant. He stopped talking again as his focus retreated to some inner horizon only he could see.

"Talk to me," I directed. "To keep your friend alive, tell his story. Age?"

"Twenty-four."

"Name?"

"Same like my father — Achmed."

"Tell me about Achmed," I said. "How did you know him? What was he like?"

Slowly, painfully, he began to tell the story of his friendship with Achmed. He spoke of their schooldays together and how, with liberation in mind, they had joined the rebel army in a pact of undying friendship of the sort that only the very young and idealistic are capable of making.

It was a long, sleepless night. It was then that I first heard of the Islamic tradition requiring the bodies of the dead to be buried within twenty-four hours of their death and as close as possible to where they died.

From a series of updates on Facebook, Yusuf learned that his friend's body had been abandoned by the retreating troops. Burial had been denied to his family by the rebels to prevent Achmed from entering into Paradise. In Islamic culture, Yusuf confided, this was just about the worst thing that could befall a person.

While it seemed unkind to deny basic dignity to a human body, I wasn't so worried about the superstitious aspects. As far as I was concerned, the soul could go where it wanted, if indeed it existed at all. I was far more horrified by the prospects of what might happen to the living than the dead. What disturbed me most were Yusuf's accounts of the treatment of prisoners. Beheadings were a common form of execution.

Yusuf was still talking when the sun came up. He was distressed by the recent uprisings in Benghazi, appalled at how the fundamentalists were trying to unsettle the city and take back territory they had lost under Gaddafi. He kept in constant touch with other Freedom Fighters via Facebook and Twitter, sending off broadsides to shake them out of their lethargy and into action. He condemned what he saw as their reluctance to continue fighting and was unable to understand it. I could. Before their day of liberation, many Libyans had little to lose. The prospects of dying may not have seemed a great price to pay for a shot at freedom. Now that they had tasted freedom and a short time of relative peace, however, they no longer wanted to risk losing their lives for a cause many felt was largely won.

I can't recall how many times Yusuf woke shivering in the night, claiming he needed his hand to be healed so he could return to Libya, insisting it was of the utmost importance for him to engage in the fight back home. Each time he spoke of it, I would try to impress on him that it was important for him to be with me and that, together, our fight from then on would be to win his personal freedom to live the life he chose. It wasn't enough for him.

ANNIVERSARY

One morning at breakfast, Yusuf made me promise to sleep over at the hotel with him the following Wednesday. He didn't say why, though he made it sound important. I was curious, but didn't ask his reasons. I was happy to spend the night with him, having no desire to go back to the lonely existence I had led prior to meeting him.

On Wednesday, I was scheduled for a group lesson followed by several one-on-one sessions, and simply stayed on at the hotel after classes. Early in the evening we went to a restaurant. Yusuf was quiet and pensive all through the meal. After a light supper of some of his favorite dishes, *shish tawouk* and *moutabal* and some others, we walked along the street holding hands. It had become a more regular occurrence since WorldPride. It was also dark, so Yusuf didn't fear being seen as much as he might in the daytime.

Once again, he reminded me of my promise to stay with him that night. I assured him I hadn't forgot about it. I jokingly reminded him that I now had a toothbrush permanently taking up space in the bathroom drawer and was equipped to stay over whenever it suited us.

We arrived back at the hotel and joined a queue to take the elevators up to his floor.

"You must tell me what is so important today," I said at last.

"Yes, Geef, but first coming in my room."

I waited impatiently as the elevator climbed to the sixteenth floor and then as we walked together down the hallway. That night the corridor seemed excessively long.

Yusuf took a long time to settle in, offering me first chewing gum then a candy bar and finally a bottle of water as we sat side by side on his bed.

"Geef, today is anniversary of my wounding," he said at last, holding his injured hand before him. "Need to stay with Yusuf."

He seldom allowed me to see his hand without its protective covering, which he rarely removed except when bathing. I took hold of it now, carefully unwrapping the cloth and letting it fall to the floor, revealing the reddened skin grafted over the smashed and broken bone. I pressed my lips to the stubs of his fingers.

"I will always be here for you," I told him.

"You are best for me," he said. "Never forget me, Geef."

"I will never forget you, Yusuf."

We watched a bit of television, but he could barely focus. He spoke rapidly and feverishly all evening, as though to ward off the time when we would have to go to bed.

At long last, he took his medication then said his prayers and turned out the light. I heard him murmuring off and on for more than an hour while I read and kept vigil over his sleeping form.

At one point, just as I was falling asleep, he cried out, "Is coming!"

I shook him awake. "What's coming?"

He sat up, staring ahead in the darkness, clutching the blankets to his chest.

"Military is coming to kill me," he said, his eyes stark with fear, as though he actually saw them approaching.

"You're safe," I told him. "You're here with me. With Geef."

At last he seemed to realize where he was, then buried his face in my chest and sobbed loudly while I stroked his hair.

To calm him I recited some lines from a John Donne poem, *The Anniversary*, memorized during a long-ago English literature class.

> *Here upon earth we're kings, and none but we*
> *Can be such kings, nor of such subjects be.*
> *Who is so safe as we? where none can do*
> *Treason to us, except one of us two.*

The poem had seemed a promise of earthly peace and serenity, lines of reassurance spoken by a lover to his beloved. I had recited it often and in many places, sometimes silently to myself and sometimes aloud to students. What I hadn't seen at the time were the starker implications buried in those last lines. I see them now.

All of this was emotionally exhausting for both of us. Despite our deep and mutual love, it was as though we could never truly experience any long-lasting moments of peace together. The war had followed him across the sea, like an evil wind that kept scouring the earth until it found him and laid claim to him once again.

I tried to get him to go back to sleep, but there was little rest for us that night. We were still awake when the sun rose. Yusuf turned on his laptop, replying to a message from a fellow student whose treatment was over and who would be returning home the following day. The student, who had agreed to take Yusuf's suitcase full of gifts for his family, had discovered the bag was too large and needed Yusuf to repack everything in a smaller case. I said I would leave him to his task. Yusuf thanked me for having stayed with him. I left while the rest of the city was just waking to their peaceful, ordered lives.

I see now that my world was not and never could be his world. He belonged to the dust and sand, to mosques and muezzins, and a religion mired in the Middle Ages. And to war — most of all to war. He'd given his soul and body to the fighting. That was his siren's call. I was merely the distraction from his real love, fighting. I see now that he should never have come to Canada, and most of all that he should never have met me. I only dulled his thinking and threw dirt in his eyes, temporarily blinding him to all that he was, all that he so desperately needed and wanted to become.

STARS

It's nearly morning. How long have I been standing here keeping watch over this pile of stones? The moon is halfway across the sky, lighting up the shrine I have built — my monument to a doomed love.

Something scurries over my foot, startling me for an instant. It's a rat. I kick it away so that it won't get any ideas about where its breakfast is coming from. I recently read how scientists claim that after an all-out nuclear war the only survivors will be rats and cockroaches on the land, and sharks in the oceans. It's not reassuring.

Looking up, I can make out what looks like a pathway among the stars. Clouds snag briefly on those traces of light that left home thousands of years ago, emissaries from another time and place, then dance lightly away. It looks like it would be easy to climb up there and stay, lulled into a peaceful, heavenly existence. Not so down here on earth.

I like to think that one day the world will become a federation of peaceful nations, like a pathway among the stars for those who believe in the sanctity and unity of all life. Countries can opt in or out, as they wish. There won't be any pressure to join, just the promise of a life lived without fear, with international passports for those who share and respect those values. The others, those who cling to the old order of insularity and self-preservation, will maintain their borders and boundaries, fighting for power and domination, while the rest will share in all things good, passing freely from place to place. There will be no owners, just minders and keepers. Nothing to kill or die for, as someone once said. Otherwise, rats and cockroaches and sharks will inherit the earth.

CRAZY

Yusuf wasn't the only one to suffer from the devastating psychological assaults of post-traumatic stress. I discovered that, to some degree, it was shared by nearly all the men in his group. One of the more worrisome aspects of the treatment Yusuf and the others underwent was the medications they were prescribed, both for healing and to keep them dulled. One night while we were watching television in his room, Yusuf's cell rang. He answered, taking the phone with him into the next room where I heard him speaking heatedly in Arabic. At first I was worried he'd received bad news of some sort, but soon realized he was arguing with someone. He came back, gripping the phone in an agitated manner and shaking his head.

I looked at him inquisitively. He put his hand over the receiver as an angry harangue continued on the other end.

"What is it?" I asked.

He quietly explained that a friend in another hotel had run out of pain killers and was demanding that Yusuf give him some of his. The man was threatening to come and beat him up if he did not. His name was Tariq. A father of four in his early-thirties, he was homesick. He missed his family. And he was going crazy.

It sounded as though he was strung out on pills. Yusuf

asked me what he should do. I told him under no circumstances should he let an angry man, half-crazed and in pain, come over and demand pain killers. He told the man no and hung up.

Half an hour went by. We forgot about the call till a knock came at the door. Yusuf opened it. There stood another student, not one of mine. He was a short, pugnacious fellow I had seen around the meeting rooms once or twice. His right arm was amputated at the elbow. His teeth showed blackened, rotting stumps when he spoke. I saw the opiate sheen in his eyes as he came in and stormed about, shouting at Yusuf in Arabic. His anger and his appearance were alarming. It was like having an angry wasp buzzing around the room. He waved the stump of his arm, the angry purple scars offered up as Exhibit A in his campaign for more pain killers.

The shouting continued at length, though I could not understand what was said. For a moment, I considered calling hotel security. Yusuf's face had taken on a glazed look. It was the expression he wore when he wanted to avoid confrontation, with me or others. After a moment he went into the bathroom and emerged with a pill container, dumping three painkillers in Tariq's palm. The man looked down at the pills and began shouting again. Exasperated, Yusuf went back for another container and gave him two more pills, wrapping them in a napkin.

The man's mood changed suddenly. He grinned like a madman, as if it had all been for fun. Then he took off with a wave, probably to bully more drugs from his fellow students.

Yusuf looked at me sheepishly. I told him sternly that he would have to report this to the group's medical coordinator.

He shrugged and said it would be disloyal for him to inform on a friend in need.

"You're a medical student," I argued. "You know about medication. He could die from what he's doing."

He stopped to take stock of what I'd said. The thought seemed to register with him. I think at that moment, however, we were both wondering if Tariq might be better off dead. On top of everything else that had happened to him, he was now a junkie as well.

I had learned early about drugs from my peers in high school, but this kind of behavior was new to me. My addictions were simple: food and love. While I've never gone hungry, I have starved for love; it is not an enviable state. But I have never felt so strongly the urge for any physical substance that I would threaten another person with violence to get it.

Since meeting Yusuf, I had learned two Arabic words for crazy. The first, *majnoon*, is relatively harmless, but the second, which I won't repeat here, is far worse, and has sexually abusive connotations for which I never learned an exact translation. Even Yusuf didn't like it when I repeated it, which was far too often in those days.

MOTHER II

I hadn't talked to my mother for a while. That fact was made clear by the frequency of her calls, which largely went unanswered around that time. It was not that I had been consciously avoiding her so much as that my life had become uncharacteristically busy, what with tutoring and the time I was spending with Yusuf. At first, her messages were friendly, but they soon became needling and accusatory, as though I had deprived her of something vital through my lack of contact. We hardly shared scintillating conversation at the best of times, while at the worst it was fraught with confrontation on both sides. If she really needed someone to talk to, I thought, she should hire a shrink. When my father died, she was left with a decent income. It was up to her to spend it in ways that would help her enjoy her life — or not — just as she pleased.

"Why don't you take a trip?" I suggested, on one of the few occasions when we spoke in real time.

She claimed to be tired of travelling — earlier in the year she'd gone to France, the previous year to Switzerland, followed by a week with her sister in Manchester. I could hardly sympathize. Before I met Yusuf there was little I liked better than to travel. Some people enjoy pricey wine in dark bars on the Left Bank, while others prefer good food on spectacular coastlines overlooking the Mediterranean. I have always needed the rush of newness, the feel of unknown winds on my face, with the possibility of an adventure to come around every corner. True, it has hampered my ability to accept what I referred to as "the mundane world." But I had long since known and accepted that particular failing in myself. While some might say it was the cause of my undoing, I would say, rather, even at this late hour amidst the mounting evidence of all I have done wrong, that it has been my salvation.

One morning early I called her. Our conversation was brief. What had I been doing with my time? How was the tutoring going? What of future plans? It was her mini-inquisition disguised as motherly concern. I answered without interest, giving little of myself away, having become adept at hiding in plain sight. It was only when she persisted in cross-examining me that I let slip I was dating.

Suddenly, there were expectations. She hoped for my sake that it was someone who could offer me a good future, someone well educated and of the "right" class. I felt a rank bitterness rising from my depths, firstly that she would presume to have a say in whom I might see and, secondly, that there was a "right" class of human being when the subject was love. From the little I've experienced of it, love cuts across all human-made distinctions such as class or race. I've felt as joyous rolling in the hay with the eldest son of a poor family in Portugal as sleeping on silk sheets with a minor member of British royalty, having unashamedly done both in my time.

I suspect it was borne of my intention to outrage her that I proceeded to tell her about Yusuf and of my hopes to help him obtain citizenship. Her pronouncement that he did not sound like a suitable match for me on any level pretty much ended the conversation. I resented her judgement. Once again we were at that old impasse: we disagreed on the most fundamental principles of life. I had begun to love him with an agonizing fierceness, a passion that was at times painful, and knew that I would not tolerate anyone's disapproval of him.

I recalled David's whimsical but entirely apt advice, offered at some point in our friendship: if you're going to have parents, then you must take the time to train them properly. Only by then it was too late. I was never able to train mine in any socially redeeming way.

The conversation that day concluded to our mutual dissatisfaction. A draw, as it were. I had learned by then not to give up the fight as long as my mother held the advantage; otherwise, I would feel I had walked away from her minus my pride, a prospect I considered dismal at best and untenable at worst.

This time there were no attempts made to placate my anger, no suggestions of going out to celebrate. What would we have had to celebrate? I was dating one of my students, who was a potential refugee from a foreign country. Looked at from my mother's point of view, it was just one more instance of where I had failed to live up to my potential. Nor was there any mention of going to visit my father's grave together. Even this fallback had failed.

PHILOSOPHY

For a long time after I graduated, I still thought fondly of my early days at university. I was fresh out of high school when I first arrived in the realms of academia and found the world beginning to open up to me, offering what seemed like a place of promise and hope. My head was in the clouds and, soon enough, my feet were over someone else's shoulders as I discovered the twin delights of sex and what I took for deep philosophical thinking shared with my peers, though with hindsight I came to realize these thoughts were in reality a compendium of clichéd teenage ramblings and half-baked opinions.

I am now older and arguably wiser, but for a while university seemed to be the place I had been destined to reach for much of my life to that point. As I said earlier, I believed that character was destiny; I had entered what I came to think of as the Realm of Choice. If university was a world of new companions, open-minded thinking, and experimentation, then best of all — or so it seemed at the time — it also offered me freedom from the constraints of family.

It wasn't long before disillusionment once more took hold, however, and I concluded that all human relationships eventually lead to disappointment. My new friends were not so bold or committed as I had first thought. They were just young and idealistic, making the same mistakes all humans make, idealizing professors who should never have been put on pillars, while subjecting their peers to scorn and ridicule for not sharing their beliefs.

I was to experience a similar disappointment in affairs of the heart when I met the only other person I have felt as obsessive about as I have with Yusuf. I'd had sex with men by then, but I had never fully explored the realms of love. I was about to discover it.

When we met, Herbert was a star wrestler and all-round jock from the prairies. As he told it, he had his first sexual experience with a cousin in his uncle's barn at the age of eight. Once hooked, he never stopped exploring the possibilities open to a young man of good looks and athletic build. To my mind, the prairies had always seemed a wasteland of wheat fields and potash. By the time Herbert finished telling me of his youthful adventures in the land of ravenous farmers, however, I had begun to envision it as some sort of boundless sexual playground.

Before meeting Herbert, I'd looked for ways to explore my sexual urges quietly, without pursuing the possibilities openly. In fact, I was still operating under the assumption that one day I would marry a woman and together we would start a family. I remember the day I glimpsed a vision of a different future altogether. I was in the school cafeteria when I became aware of the presence of a star athlete whose reputation was well-known to many. His name and picture had been in the papers. So I felt a jolt when he lumbered over to my table and sat across from me, leaving me to wonder if I was about to be humiliated in some arcane way I had yet to fathom. His smile was dazzling as he said hello. I mumbled a greeting then turned away to focus on the tasteless mound of lasagna on my plate.

Knowing his reputation as the star jock, I assumed he had sat with me because of a lack of seating, but when I looked around I realized there were plenty of other spots he could have chosen. From time to time I caught him watching me, but I did not return his stare. I finished my lunch but, curious, lingered over coffee so I could be near him. Not wanting him to guess my motive, however, I made a show of watching a female student at the next table.

After a moment, Herbert leaned toward me and said in a mocking tone, "Why are you watching her when you could be watching me?"

"Excuse me?" I mumbled, spilling coffee onto the table top.

"You heard me," he said. "I could do a lot more for you than she could."

By late afternoon, I had to admit that Herbert could indeed do whatever it was he did to my complete and utter satisfaction. It was not only his reputation that was stellar. His cock was too.

I was in bliss. But bliss inevitably fades. Sometimes it leads to love, which leads again to all the disappointments relationships bring. Ours lasted two months, during which I would wait outside his classrooms and follow him to and from the gym like a faithful puppy. I was completely smitten. Being a star means you have many fans, however, and fans must be kept happy. And, as happens with many youthful infatuations, this one led first to the Land of Merry but ended abruptly as

Herbert found another fascination, another lover to follow him around, leaving me consigned to the Land of the Lost.

In the meantime, I had learned what it was I wanted: men. And that revelation led me to believe, wrongly as it turned out, that I was making an important life choice. Genetically speaking, the choice had already been made for me. It was biology, not character, that won the battle to shape my destiny in the sexual realms, although this was not something I would fully understand until later.

With Herbert behind me, I soon turned to other lovers while yet again wondering about the choices I seemed to be making. Why did so-and-so's smile turn me on enough for me to make the first move rather than wait for him to do it, or why could another man thrill me to no end in bed when he might be nowhere near as good-looking as one whose sexual advances I had just turned down without a second thought?

It was Kierkegaard who famously suggested that life was best understood when viewed backwards, but appending that gloomy prognostication with the acknowledgment that it still must be lived forwards. At this late stage in the game, for what it's worth, I find myself in full agreement.

Besides my infatuation with Herbert and his all-star cock, I also recall the jejune discussions among my fellow freshmen held around that time in our Introduction to Psychology class. "Choice and Destiny" was the topic one warm spring afternoon, and the professor was doing his best to sound as though our discussion was fresh to his ears.

A boy named Pete, a ladies' man with floppy blonde hair, spoke up.

"I often ponder things like this," he said pompously. "I sometimes wonder what would happen if I chose to come to school tomorrow by following an alternate route — say, via Route B instead of the more direct Route A, which I normally take. How would that change my destiny?"

"You would get here later," I joked, to no one else's amusement but my own. These were supposed to be serious talks, after all.

"Seriously," Pete persisted. "My life could change drastically if I took one route instead of another. The problem is, how do you know which route leads to fulfillment and satisfaction and which route leads to ruin?"

"Try it tomorrow and let us know," someone else suggested.

"'Two roads converged in a snowy woods'," said I. "'And that has made all the difference.'"

One and all, my classmates turned a deaf ear to my finely tuned love of poetics.

Not to be put off, I continued. "The truth is you would still end up here at Philosophy 101, unless of course you randomly got hit by a car while travelling on Route B, in which case it wouldn't matter much."

I hadn't spoken up often in class till then, so the others stopped to listen while I held the airwaves.

"Or else Pete would get distracted by a blonde instead of a brunette, which is his usual taste," I continued, sending up his theorizing.

Thanks to Herbert, I had just had my heart broken for the first time and was still hurt and angry about it. What difference could choosing Route B over Route A make? Life was crap and

I was alone. Worse, I couldn't tell anyone about it, because I had no friends who knew I was queer.

"You may as well theorize that nothing exists unless you can see it, though you'll never be able to prove it," someone else chimed in.

"I can prove it," I said.

"How?" demanded several other students.

Our professor smiled and looked on while surreptitiously checking his watch.

"Make a phone call to your mother and wait to see if she answers. You can't see her, but if she answers she exists," I replied, to great guffaws.

The laughter went on as I continued. By now I had their full attention.

"Here's a challenge," I said. "Name all the things you believe in even though you know they're not real."

"The Easter Bunny," someone called out.

"Santa Claus," said another, getting into the game.

The girl beside me turned to me. "What about you?"

"Love," I said.

All I remember is that the room got quiet. Then someone called me a spoilsport. After a while, the conversation continued without me. I don't remember if I was actually being serious that day. Now, it's probably the only thing I believe in.

COPY/PASTE

It was around this time that I took it on myself to introduce David and Yusuf to one another. They were the two people I was closest to, so it only made sense for me to bring them together, although I did not do so lightly or without a great deal of forethought.

The truth is I was apprehensive about this potential meeting even before it was set up. Both knew of the other's existence, of course, as I had talked about each to the other on occasion. David, for his part, always got the lowdown on my lovers sooner or later, while Yusuf was aware of everyone in my life by dint of how much time we spent together. So in a sense they knew one another in advance. I took some comfort in that.

I thought a coffeehouse best for the meeting, something nondescript in decor and neutral in its associations, as far as that was possible to find. I chose a little place called the Bulldog Café, where the staff were supercilious enough to ignore the patrons, apart from taking orders and accepting tips.

At the hotel, I watched Yusuf dress nervously for the meeting, trying on one shirt after another while asking my opinion of each choice before ignoring what I said. This, of course, was followed closely by the ritual dousing in Calvin Klein *Sport* until I groused that we would be late if we didn't leave immediately.

David was already seated when we arrived. On entering, Yusuf looked around the café with suspicion, as he often did on encountering a new space. Perhaps it was a habit formed during the war, when any unknown territory needed to be assessed for potential dangers before entering rather than simply taking for granted that whatever it held was safe. Who am I to say, never having done anything remotely brave in my entire life?

There was a moment of discomfort on both their parts as they shook hands awkwardly. I watched David surreptitiously take in Yusuf's damaged beauty, his long hair and hardened features. I was, in fact, having an attack of nerves wondering what his assessment would be later that evening, already half dreading what I would hear the moment he got me alone. If I could have turned around and marched out of the café right then, I would have.

What went through Yusuf's head in those moments, I never learned. I sent him to the counter with our orders, hoping to deflect anything negative David might have to say in those initial moments. Quite uncharacteristically, however, my outspoken friend kept any judgements he had to himself.

Yusuf returned with a tray of coffee then sat directly across from David. All the while, I kept wishing I had never set up the date. Until that moment, anything they said or felt about each other was simply the result of impressions filtered from one to the other by me. After this meeting, all would be concrete. It would matter. If they decided they hated each other, then it was something I would have to deal with. I was aware of the risk I had taken in bringing them together. From that point on, it would prove impossible for me to navigate between the two relationships if they actively disliked one another.

There is nothing so awkward as an unwanted silence. Outside the window, the clouds rolled by on what was an otherwise calm and peaceful day. Cars drove past on the street, cyclists stopped and chained their bikes to the railing outside the shop. I waited for someone to speak.

The awkwardness dissipated quickly, as neither nature nor David can abide a vacuum. Words began to fill the space around us and the afternoon unfolded smoothly from then on, albeit with David doing most of the talking. He was careful not to stray from safe territory, most of it pertaining to our newly reclaimed friendship. Perhaps he realized that Yusuf held the trump in any turf war — my love for him. Or perhaps there was more than I had imagined in those unspoken thoughts I could feel roiling inside his head whenever he turned and looked in my direction.

Having got used to being the one who did most of the talking during tutoring sessions, I was more than happy to let someone else take over in the downtime. David was always ready to oblige. I've never truly understood if his compulsive chattiness has to do with nervousness or simply a desire to take over any situation he finds himself in. It strikes me as equal parts annoying and comforting. I've had friends declare him the most entertaining person they'd ever met, while others claimed him to be a total bore. To each his own. Yusuf, of course, had a hard time keeping up with David's breakneck pace of speaking as he dispensed advice and consolation for the miseries of war, emigration, the studying of foreign languages, and missing his family back home, but he did his best.

Through all this, I still had no sense from Yusuf what impressions might have been forming in his head regarding this hurricane-force of a man seated before him in the flesh. I gulped my coffee as my apprehension grew.

During a break in the conversation he turned to me and, with a nod, said, "Have a big heart, this man." It was his highest compliment.

I saw a look of bashful astonishment cross David's face. Although he persists in presenting a cynical outlook to the world, every now and then a few perceptive souls are able to discern the real David, the sensitive David beneath the voluble exterior. As it turned out, Yusuf was one of these.

He turned to me. "This same like my cousin."

"You mean David looks like your cousin?" I asked.

"Yes! Exactly same. Look, talk, everything. Like copy/paste."

We laughed at Yusuf's use of computer functions to compare David with his cousin who, like many men in Libya, was in the military. I think it was at that moment that David's perception of Yusuf began to come into view clearly. I can't say exactly what it was, but there was a change in the atmospheric pressure surrounding us, as though two potential opponents had decided to take off the gloves and place some sort of trust in one another.

It was also then that Yusuf was inspired to open up about his war experiences. He spoke of driving an ambulance, of risking his life to pick up wounded soldiers in the desert and bring them to safety. Mostly, he spoke of his passion for liberating his country from the twin yokes of tyranny and oppression, and of helping better the lives of the poor and illiterate. For the first time, I heard him describe in detail the accident that cost him part of his hand and damaged a foot. Clearly, he felt David merited special attention.

He'd been driving along an open road in the desert, he said, when a rocket hit the passenger side of the ambulance, tossing him clear just before the vehicle exploded and burned. He'd been left for dead, crawling on hands and knees to a nearby encampment where astonished rebel soldiers helped him to safety. Months spent recuperating in hospital ended with his being selected to join the small group of rebel fighters sent abroad for reconstructive surgery. This would be no simple copy/paste operation, but a highly complex procedure aimed at creating a state-of-the-art prosthetic hand for him when he was done. It was also the first time he had spoken in depth about the procedures that lay ahead for him.

Yusuf spoke for half an hour while David listened intently to his tales of war. I can't recall any other time in our decade-long friendship when David sat so patiently and silently while another person spoke of his experiences. I doubt that even I have held his attention for such a considerable length of time.

Finally, Yusuf's story came to an end. David nodded, but said nothing. The sheer hazardousness of Yusuf's tale alone would have given pause to many. His willingness to attempt it in English was not without its merits also, and he'd handled it commendably. Then, as suddenly as it began, the conversation turned to other things, to worlds far away from Yusuf's past. I hesitantly brought up the subject of helping Yusuf get citizenship papers. Still, David said nothing.

The café was closing. The staff buzzed around, making sure the lingering clients knew their time was up and that any procrastination would not be tolerated. We finished our drinks and were getting ready to depart. Yusuf went to the bathroom. It was then that David turned to me. He sighed and seemed unable to speak. For a moment he seemed like an older, wiser person wanting desperately to impart wisdom to a younger friend who might potentially be unable to comprehend the depth of his message. I dreaded his pronouncement, whatever it might be.

Then he said simply, "I say this against my better judgement. However, I understand now why you love him."

RAMADAN

One morning I opened my eyes to an ungodly racket. Yusuf was squatting in the middle of the room, not far from the bed. I blinked and tried to make out what he was doing. Then it dawned on me: calisthenics.

"Good morning, honey," he called out between squats, his arms outstretched.

I laughed, knowing how he loved to ape North American idioms as though they might help him assimilate into the modern world, like donning a suit jacket over a thobe robe. The results were often a confusion of styles, just as Yusuf's thinking was confused on many fronts. Even more than I could contemplate, as it turned out, though I still hadn't given up trying to make him see my point of view.

I rolled onto my side and pulled a pillow over my head, but it couldn't drown out the shrill sounds coming from his laptop.

"Geef, wake up!"

Eventually I gave up the struggle. Before long we both were standing upright in the cramped room, performing exercises like army commandoes to the buzzing and rattling of traditional Arabic music sung by a singer with the voice of a goat herder and accompanied by an instrument that sounded like a dentist's drill.

The singer, Yusuf informed me, called himself Max Libya. He was a national hero among the young. He was rumored to be gay and for this he had been beaten by the police during Gaddafi's regime. Known for his long hair, his head had been shorn by the officers who assaulted and threw him into a cell. Undaunted, Max took his complaint to the Human Rights commission. Since then, Yusuf proudly declared, no one had been able to touch him. The instrument contributing to the din, I learned, was an oud. And while the music might have had an appeal to goats, it had none for me.

Yusuf laughingly related how a friend of his had hired Max to sing at his wedding, paying him $2000 for a single appearance. He was a very good belly dancer, Yusuf related. So good, in fact, that the female wedding guests were all jealous of him.

Ramadan had just started. It was a traditional month of fasting to commemorate the first revelation of the Quran to the Prophet Mohammad. Any and all sensual practices were put aside, including sex with one's spouse. Food was to be taken only after sundown. While I could imagine going without food for a month, the thought of a month without sex gave me pause. But if Yusuf could do it then so could I.

That year, Canada Day fell during the first week of Ramadan. While Yusuf acquainted me with his cultural observances, I continued my campaign to expose him to modern values and traditions. I decided to bring him down to the waterfront for the fireworks display, something I normally would have yawned over but now considered an opportunity to tell him more about this country that I hoped he would eventually adopt. Since we wouldn't be having sex, I thought it would also help while away the time together.

Tuesday evening, we wandered down to the beach. Rainbow Pride flags were still displayed all along the street. The more the merrier, I told myself.

Neither of us had eaten all day, in accordance with custom, as I had decided to observe Ramadan along with him.

"Geef, you are best for me," he replied, when I said I would also abstain from food.

I had not, however, fully considered Yusuf's psychological state when I suggested we take in the celebrations at the waterfront. Nor had I told him what to expect, other than throngs of excited people everywhere. The fireworks had not yet begun when we arrived, but there was a sense of expectation in the air. Within minutes, the first shots went off overhead, the explosions booming in our ears as streamers of color unfurled above.

I glanced over in anticipation of his surprised look of pleasure. Instead, his face had taken on a fearful expression.

He gripped my arm. "Geef, this is like explosion in my ambulance," he said.

Instantly, I realized what I had done, plunging him right back in the midst of the war. I shepherded him as quickly as I could through the crowds, which were substantial by then, and we headed back uptown. I tried to distract him along the way, but it was useless. He covered his ears and shivered with each successive barrage. By the time we reached his hotel, he was nearly crazed with the explosions bursting above.

That night, when the display was finally over, he kept going out to stand on the balcony and gaze over the skyline before returning inside the room. Every few minutes he repeated the action. It was as if he expected the war to return. It had become almost an obsession. I was fearful for him.

At ten o'clock, a knock came at his door. He called out and someone yelled back in Arabic. Then he turned to me.

"Geef, is time for Ramadan meal," he said with relief. "I coming back. You wait?"

I nodded. "Yes, I will wait for you here."

"Please," he said with a hesitant glance, as though he feared I might disappear before he returned.

I turned on television to pass the time. It was the usual parade of bad news and venal politicians saying insipid things to ensure the citizenry that all was well with the world and they could safely go back to their consumerist oblivion and their unconscious lives.

I was nearly asleep when Yusuf returned carrying a plate heaped with food for me. He looked pleasantly surprised to find me still there.

"I told you I would wait," I reminded him.

"Yes, I know."

I ate ravenously while he described supper with his fellow Libyans, how they had exchanged news of their medical reports, upcoming operations and treatments, and of the ongoing fighting back home. And family. Always family. Before which nothing took precedence except Allah.

When I finished eating, Yusuf asked me to write a Ramadan note to post on Facebook. I was used to his requests to write these notes, which I'd been penning for some time. This time I made him write it, only correcting his spelling and grammar.

Dear parents, he wrote. *I am doing well here in my new home and making progress with my healing. I hope you are enjoying peace and happiness back in Libya. Happy Ramadan. Your obedient son, Yusuf.*

It was nearly midnight. We had been sitting side by side at the computer table for a quarter hour working out the wording of his short note when I felt his leg brush against mine. I didn't resist when he leaned toward me and gave me a long, deeply-felt kiss.

His breathing came heavily to my ears. I pointed up to the ceiling and said, "No sex."

He smiled and asked if I would stay the night. I said no, but that I would see him tomorrow. For once he didn't complain or pout. We watched more television and talked a while longer. When I next looked at his bedside clock, it said one-forty. I asked if that was the correct time. He nodded.

"Time goes fast with Geef," he said.

I stretched out on the bed and said I had changed my mind and would stay the night with him.

"You see?" I told him. "You ask, 'Geef, will you do this? Geef will you do that?' And I do it. I don't like to say 'no' to you."

He laughed happily. I slept with him folded in my arms. Halfway through the night, I felt his erection forcing its way between my legs. I made him put on a condom before he entered me. With his face crushed against my neck, I heard him mumble the word "forever."

As he came, he cried out, "Need Geef! Need everything with Geef."

Fool that I am, I thought I had won the battle for his soul.

BETRAYAL

The crisis came sooner rather than later. I see now that it was sheer delusion on my part to think it would never happen. In fact, it should have been apparent to anyone with an objective eye, but then I've never been good at viewing life objectively.

In all this time, I hadn't lost sight of the fact that Yusuf's prime objective was to undergo medical treatment. The chief impairment lay with his left hand. He'd already had two minor operations since I met him, and was anxiously waiting for the doctors to begin the painstaking measurements and calculations to outfit him with a prosthetic replacement. For a while he was excited by the prospect of this cutting-edge technology being designed for him, buoyed by the thought of having a set of mechanical fingers that would obey neural impulses from his brain and enable him to perform highly dexterous tasks. In time, the experts assured, this would restore to him the use of both hands, but it couldn't happen until the doctors declared his wounds completely healed. The process was slow, hampered by microscopic bits of shrapnel lodged in his flesh.

For the first month I knew him, he kept his damaged hand carefully concealed under a heavy gauze bandage, even at night when we slept together. Gradually, however, he began to relax and allowed me to see the wound, the stubs where his fingers had been, the angry red weal of flesh alongside the lone thumb that looked like something left behind.

To make things worse, he often walked in public with a careless disregard, swinging his arms about him. More than once he returned to the hotel complaining of having hurt himself by knocking his hand against a telephone pole or parking meter. Admonishing him for his carelessness had no effect.

I, too, was beginning to worry over the slowness of his recovery, especially because of the large amount of antibiotics being pumped into his system. I disliked how he would go for long periods of time without eating, complaining that his stomach was in turmoil due to his medication. As well, there was the added worry over how he had abused his body by accidentally consuming far too many drugs before I bought him a pill counter.

Being foggy-headed from sedatives and painkillers often prevented him from remembering to do the exercises necessary to keep the nerves in his hand limber. One morning, as he unwrapped the dressing, I heard him give a moan of distress. Looking over, I saw that his thumb had turned a deep purple.

"What happened?" I asked, frightened by the sight. "Did you hurt yourself?"

He shook his head. "No, not hurt. Forget to exercise. Maybe sleep on my hand."

"You need to go to the hospital and get it looked at."

He shook his head. "No, Geef. Not telling doctor. I am bad, not looking after my wound."

I was insistent. "You need to go to the hospital."

For once, rather than argue, he agreed to compromise. He would call his health practitioner and inform her of what had happened. If she asked to see him, he would go to the hospital, but he made it clear he would do this alone.

Yusuf's English was improving, but I knew he still struggled with words. More than once I suggested that he put me in touch with his doctor in case he needed help with his home-care regime. Always, he refused. With time I became more adamant, however, especially at moments like these.

"What if you get the directions wrong?" I persisted. "You could jeopardize the healing process."

He put his hand on his heart. "Geef, you are best for me, for sex and everything. But not for this."

"I can help you," I insisted. "If you have questions for the doctors, I can make sure you understand the answers fully."

This just annoyed him.

"No, Geef. Then they think we are more than friends."

"But we *are* more than friends," I countered.

He glowered. "Not for Muslim. I cannot."

The argument was always circular, especially when it led to situations like the one he found himself in that day. I felt helpless at being kept in the dark about his medical care. I didn't want our disagreements to worry him unduly, but I never gave up trying to convince him.

One of Yusuf's problems came from a quarter I hadn't fully recognized till then. His fellow student, Abdel, was older than the rest of the men and looked on as a hero by the others. He'd risked his life during a crucial battle, delivering his small, rag-tag army to a victory that helped liberate a small town and put it in the hands of the Freedom Fighters. To many, his bravery was legendary. And what's more, he had the video footage to prove it.

As well as being a mushroom farmer, Abdel was also an avid videographer. Prior to the war he'd been accomplished at his art, accumulating a good deal of sophisticated equipment. When the war started, Abdel and his camera became inseparable.

Although I was his teacher, I had not been able to crack Abdel's shell and get close to him. He was extremely private and independent. One day several months into my tutoring sessions, after considerable urging on Yusuf's part, Abdel invited us both up to his room. When we got there, he was in bed with the curtains drawn. His wheelchair had been folded and leaned against the far wall. A new motorized scooter blocked the entryway. Yusuf and I made our way around it to enter.

As a double-amputee, Abdel was accorded greater care and consideration in the hotel, including having his meals in bed if he chose. He was also a heavy smoker. Despite the prohibition on cigarettes, the air was dense with his smoking. The room was a foul mess, with empty food containers dropped on the floor beside the waste basket.

I looked around for a place to sit, but the only chair had used clothing piled on it. Instead, I sat on the window ledge, gazing down at the street while Yusuf and Abdel spoke to one another in Arabic.

There was a good deal of discussion between them, accompanied by considerable grumbling on Abdel's part. I couldn't tell what was going on, other than that Yusuf was pleading with him to do something.

Eventually, Abdel brought out a laptop from a drawer beside the bed. Pushing aside empty juice cartons and a meal tray, he set it up on a retractable table.

Yusuf called to me excitedly to come and watch. I made my way over. The screen showed hand-held video footage of a street in what I assumed was Libya. Both the camera and its operator seemed to be watching and waiting.

This was the war in Benghazi, Yusuf explained of the furtive on-screen movements. Suddenly, I understood why I was there, what Yusuf had been begging Abdel to show us.

It was harrowing to watch. No fictionalized depiction of war on film has ever come close to what I saw shot on that hand-held camera. It wasn't over the top, as you might expect, but rather eerily ordinary. There was no great offensive, no gathering of courage before the onslaught, and no swelling soundtrack urging the actors onward. Rather, there was the silence of an everyday street at midday, broken by an occasional shout or crack of a rifle, while the camera jerked and swayed as Abdel followed the action. The men also were ordinary-looking, and young, dressed in baseball caps, T-shirts and jeans, as they hovered in and out of the camera's range. I heard mumbled conversations, low and unhurried, in the background. It was, in fact, the ordinariness that got to me, gripping in the slow, tortured moments as we waited.

Then, suddenly, from a distance came the sound of repeated gunshots and the noise of men running, followed by a terrifying scream up close. The camera jerked and fell with a jarring thud, rolling across the ground as it picked up everything in its path in one long, mad scramble — men, walls, cars, the street, the sky — as though the world had gone insane. This was followed by a heart-pounding, three-second blackout. Then, amazingly, the scene snapped back into view with the lens focused on the camera operator's leg — Abdel's leg — split open and bleeding profusely. In the background, a keening noise continued that I eventually identified as coming from Abdel.

Even when his fellow Freedom Fighters came to drag him away, Abdel would not give up the camera, filming every aspect of his rescue, from being picked up bodily to being placed in the ambulance, relinquishing it only when he was injected with a sedative and the camera was unresistingly taken from his hands. The last shot was of a bewildered medical attendant staring into the lens, trying to locate the off switch before it went black again.

I knew I had just been to the heart of war. It was a place I never wanted to see first-hand, if I had any choice in the matter.

It was only later, when we were alone back in Yusuf's room, that I heard the full story. Yusuf recounted how the doctors had tried to save Abdel's legs, only to be thwarted by recurring infections again and again until one day, fed up with their efforts, Abdel ordered them to amputate both legs above the knee.

The doctors argued: it would be better to wait till his wounds healed naturally, they said. Creating artificial limbs without his knee joints would further limit his mobility. But Abdel would not relent.

"I don't need legs to grow mushrooms," he insisted with a terrible, implacable logic.

He wasn't going to waste years of his life recuperating from the ongoing infection. He didn't want to be there. He missed his family. He wanted them to cut off the portion of his legs that were slowing his progress, even if it meant reduced mobility in future.

Abdel got his way; the doctors accepted his decision. He underwent the operation. Afterwards, his recovery sped up as far as the infection went. To his fellow veterans, and to Yusuf in particular, this seemed a victory. Abdel had taken fate into his own hands, gambled and, seemingly, won.

SUICIDE

Abdel's decision had a profound effect on Yusuf. Though generally good-natured, Yusuf was inclined to be impulsive and moody. I attributed this largely to his excessive medication as much as to the trauma he'd suffered. I never thought it might also be a part of his basic personality, but in fact it probably was that as much as anything that made him declare his impatience with the slowness of his healing. He longed to be done with his treatment, he told me. He was tired of waiting for the doctors and the drugs to fix him. He'd lost faith in them, as Abdel had. Or perhaps he just wanted to prove his own bravado.

I reasoned with him, repeating all the usual platitudes. These things take time. You can't rush healing. You're a medical student; you should know this. Nothing would pacify him, however. Night after night, whenever I stayed at the hotel, I watched as he replayed the images of the ongoing struggle in Libya on his laptop, sending out messages of hope and encouragement to those still involved in the fighting. For my part, I had yet to accept that his most ardent desire was to return to the war. From everything I had seen and heard from him, it didn't make sense.

It was around this time that he first expressed a desire to have the doctors amputate his hand, as they had done with

Abdel's legs. He had had a bad week, complaining that his hand ached non-stop for days at a time, despite the medication. He was growing impatient. More importantly, he insisted, he needed to get back to Libya to help in the war effort.

My heart skipped a beat to hear him say these things. I gave him a look I hoped would let him know I thought he was crazy or delusional.

"Yusuf," I said sternly, watching his moody, haunted eyes swing toward me. "You made a brave decision to help others during the civil war. Now make one to help yourself. Allow yourself the proper time to heal. That means staying here and not going back home. The best thing you can do is declare that you are gay and let me marry you or at least apply to stay here as a refugee."

He glared at me. "Geef, you not understand. I give my hand for this war. I give my best friends for this war. I have go back to my country!"

I shook my head at the sheer incomprehensibility of it. The truth is, I knew that nothing I had done in my life was in any way remotely meaningful compared to Yusuf's selfless actions. But at that moment I would not give him credit for how he felt, because I knew it would only encourage him to leave Canada and, at the same time, abandon me.

"You have only one hand. You're no good to anybody back home."

I said it in spite and regretted it as soon as the words were out.

"I am good for my country!" he insisted angrily.

I shook my head, but this only enraged him.

"Geef, you not understand. I have this feeling very strong I must free Libya."

"It's stupid to live for causes," I told him. "You have to live to make a better future for yourself. For both of us. This is your country now."

But, really, who was I to tell him what his future should be? Simple questions don't always beget simple answers.

"I understand what you must be feeling," I continued. "I will do anything to help, but please don't do this. Be patient. Wait till you are properly healed."

His expression darkened. "You want do something for Yusuf? Then find wife for marry me, Geef."

We were back to that old argument. I shook my head impatiently.

"You won't find a woman to marry you."

Even under heavy sedation, his eyes blazed. "Then tomorrow I tell doctor cut it off."

He made an angry gesture, as if to be free of his injured hand.

"You're being ridiculous," I told him. I got up and went to the door. "I'm going home. I don't want to hear from you again until you agree that you will not do this to yourself."

"Why, Geef? Why? Need to help Yusuf."

His pleading nearly broke me, but I felt I knew better.

"It's like you're giving up the fight," I told him.

"I don't give up ever!" He spat the words in fury.

I walked to the door and turned to look at him. "Don't call me. I don't want to hear from you until you decide not to do this."

I left him there and took a cab home. I didn't hear from him the rest of the day. The following morning, Tuesday, I woke late. I had slept badly. When I checked my phone, I saw he'd sent a text: *You are my best friend, Geef. I wighting for you. Don't let me down.*

I'm ashamed to say I let my anger get the better of me. I didn't call him back. Instead, I turned off my phone for the entire day. The following morning, I saw he'd called five times that night between 3:10 a.m. and 5:48 a.m. When I finally returned his call, there was no answer. I left a brief message saying only that I'd got his text from the previous day.

I heard nothing from him till late in the afternoon. When he called again, he sounded otherworldly and said that he hadn't slept since our argument. I thought it an exaggeration, knowing his propensity for drama. We spoke briefly then I excused myself and said I was about to begin a class. He mumbled an apology for disturbing me.

The class was a write-off. My thoughts returned to Yusuf again and again. In the evening, he called to say he'd been admitted to the psychiatric unit in the hospital. When asked what the problem was, he had told the doctors he couldn't sleep because his friend wouldn't talk to him and he was feeling suicidal. With a chill, I thought back to the many times I had seen him hanging over the balcony railing at the hotel, wondering what had been going through his mind. Now I knew. And I had been self-righteous in his hour of need.

For two days, I was unable to see him while the doctors kept him under intense observation. When he called again to say he was still in hospital but feeling a bit better, I wept.

He was finally allowed visitors. I showed up a little after ten that morning. We cried and hugged. It felt convulsive. I said I was a bad friend, saying how sorry I was and that I never wanted to hurt him. I tried to explain how his decision to ask the doctors to amputate his hand upset me. I didn't browbeat him. Mostly, I let him talk and tell me how awful it had been for him without my support.

The following day, I met him at the hospital and returned with him to the hotel. He managed to control himself in the taxi and riding in the elevator, right up until the moment we got inside his room. Then he closed the door and threw his arms around me.

"Geef, I love you too much!"

He trembled and began to sob, reminding me this was the first time he had fallen in love with a man and how difficult everything was for him without his family and friends at his side.

He told me how he'd stood on the balcony all night long, waiting for me to respond to his text. Thoughts of suicide had plagued him. All through the war his only thought had been to survive. Suddenly, he wanted to die. I held him hard against me and told him that if he ever intended to kill himself then he should kill me first, because if he died I would die too.

I took his injured hand in mine, wrapping my fingers around his. I promised him I would be his hand, his strength, and that I would always be there for him. No other promise has ever meant so much to me.

Without thinking, we ended up in bed. I straddled him as he pulled his sweatpants down and entered me with a soft moan.

After all the convulsive emotions of the past few days, I didn't stop to think that we weren't using a condom. I loved the feel of him inside me, raising and lowering myself on him. And I, a veteran and survivor of so many wars of love and sex, let him come inside me.

Looking back now, I recognize the shear madness of it. Nobody in my generation had unprotected sex unless they were willing to toss in the towel and give up the refuge of safety we had all been practicing for years. To give up was to court death. Maybe it was my penance for having brought him to the brink of suicide. Little did I know there were worse things ahead for us.

I can see him now, how when he came his face strained till it took on an expression of pain or grief. Then suddenly he was gushing inside me, crying out, "Need everything with Geef!"

I had ignored his simple plea: *You are my best friend, Geef. I wighting for you. Don't let me down.* Then, looking up at me, he said those words that chilled my soul: "Geef, one day you are going to kill me."

"I would never hurt you," I protested. "I love you more than anything. You are my best friend."

How was I to know his words would prove true, and that I would ultimately be the one to betray him? In the meantime, the other matter was settled. The doctors submitted to his request. They agreed to amputate the infected parts of his hand, leaving him with little more than a stump.

DAVID II

All the while Yusuf and I were together, I was unable to overlook the pronouncements made by both David and Arraf, who declared that unless Yusuf possessed the right mental outlook he could never belong in North America. Despite the mounting evidence, I refused to accept that verdict.

One afternoon not long after I introduced them, David called to ask me to meet up with him. We found ourselves in yet another trendy dive where we drank coffee and ate salted-caramel cookies. To David, it was paradise just to sit watching all the people laughing and chatting all around us. I remarked that he should give up his bookkeeping career and open a café.

"Imagine getting to talk to people all day long about anything you wanted," I crowed. "You would be in permanent bliss."

"And I would be sick of humanity within a week," he replied, deftly closing down the subject. "Now let's get back to you. Tell me everything."

I told him about Yusuf's decision to have his hand amputated. He listened in total silence for a moment then sighed.

"Nothing you can do about it," he advised, succinctly for once. "Not if it's what he wants. I told you this already: while you may want to save him from himself, ultimately the choices he makes will be his own. You can't be both his lover and his father."

I drew a breath. I knew better than to argue with David's wisdom.

"How's the sex? Still good?"

I nodded. "Very."

He must have sensed I was holding back. He waited, watching me closely.

"But a little … unsafe," I said.

He rolled his eyes and sighed.

"It just happened once," I said.

"Do I have to give you the lecture?"

"No," I said quickly. "I know better."

"You're dealing with someone from the Third World who doesn't know the agenda. Make sure that you do. Otherwise, you will have only yourself to blame. And believe it or not, I do not enjoy saying 'I told you so' to my many friends who choose to disregard my words of wisdom and later come to regret it."

"But how do I get past his cultural upbringing in a religion that insists on making everything like it was half a millennium ago?"

He downed the dregs of his coffee, eyed me directly and launched into it.

"Okay, religion. It's like this: some imaginary guy named God had a son who was killed. And everyone felt bad about it, so they built him a church and then they built him a lot of churches, even though God never asked them to do that, and then those people who felt guilty about it have never stopped telling other people what to do ever since. The Jews have a version of it and so do the Muslims. They're all nuts."

I waited. Because there was more. There was always more with David.

"Whether you believe it or not is irrelevant. You can't measure God in human terms. I think the literalists do more harm than good, cherry-picking their way through the Bible looking for things to shore up their side of the argument, but ignoring anything that doesn't suit their needs."

I nodded. There was no sense interrupting one of his rants.

"In Yusuf's case," he continued, "you're not only dealing with Islam, but also with Islamophobia, which people like us want to deny we feel. Of course we do. Why? Because we would rather be polite and not start arguments. But like most religions it's racist, misogynistic, and homophobic. It's everything that we as good queers are against. So we want to dress it up in a nice package and say, 'Oh, religious freedom and personal choice, la-ti-da', and hope that everything is going to be all right and that it won't affect us as a nation, even though everything affects us as a nation."

"Agreed," I said.

He went on. "On the other hand, Islam is no worse than Judaism or Christianity were a few hundred years ago. Don't forget all those lovely pogroms and inquisitions and the burnings at the stake. Oh yes — and slavery. For which the Bible is a handbook. All religions go through these phases. It's why we create them — to justify our actions. It's just that Islam is going through it now. It's out of sync with our times and thus … Islamophobia."

I listened without saying anything. I noticed some of the

customers at other tables listening as well, fascinated by his words.

David licked the crumbs from his fingers. "And that's how the world got to be so fucked up. End of sermon."

OPERATION

The operation took place on a Monday. Though we argued about it repeatedly, Yusuf would not allow me to accompany him to the hospital. He claimed it would be too hard on me, although not being there proved just as hard. More than this, however, he feared having the implications of our relationship hanging over his head along with everything else he was facing.

In the end, I acquiesced and continued with my lessons, spending an hour with the perfidious Abdel — at least that was what he'd become in my mind, a dark conjurer who spirited away the rational and reasoning side of my lover. In class that day I kept stealing glances at the stumps of his legs, something I had never allowed myself to do with my students till then. I always tried to think of them as whole, despite whatever physical injuries and wounds they were suffering. But now I saw them for what they were — men whose minds and bodies had been torn and broken by war.

Abdel would never dance with his wife again. Yusuf would never perform a full surgical operation. Tariq would never fully embrace his children with both arms. It was a reality I had to accept. They already had. Feeling sorry for them would not do anyone any good.

I waited anxiously through the appointed hour then called the hospital. I was told the operation had been a success. I was of two minds about going in to see him that day, but we had agreed that I could visit once Yusuf woke from the anesthetic, after the butchering of his hand, as I had come to think of it, was complete.

Yusuf had also made me promise not to talk to his Muslim brothers if I ran into any of them at the hospital. If I did meet anyone, I was to say I was a representative of his father's company back home. I didn't understand the need for the elaborate lie, but I didn't argue. I had no intention of betraying his wishes. What I hadn't bargained on was being grilled by someone with ulterior motives.

He was asleep when I arrived. I sat beside him, not daring to touch the tightly bandaged hand that was laid carefully across his chest. It looked much smaller than it had the night before. His other hand, the good one, was tucked beneath the covers on the far side of the bed where I couldn't grasp it, though I longed to do so.

From time to time Yusuf's eyelids flickered, but they didn't open. I could only guess what dreams or nightmares he was having, and whether I might appear in time to kill the scorpion in some new garden. When a nurse came to check on him, I asked how the operation had gone. She smiled unconvincingly and said it had gone well.

"Are you family?" she asked.

"Yes," I said, before I could stop myself.

She gave me a look that said she found my answer suspect at best.

"Friend of the family, I mean."

She looked down at the clipboard attached to his bed, hummed and hawed a moment, then smiled again.

"All good," she said, before ducking out of the room.

I had been there for maybe an hour when I heard footsteps in the hall. I looked up to see a young man with the tell-tale facial hair of a practicing Muslim enter the room. He was dressed in a casual suit and tie, complete Western garb. His eyes were cold and glittery. He did not look like a Freedom Fighter. Nor had I seen him around at the hotel where most of the other Libyans lived.

"How is he?" he asked in English that held no trace of an accent.

"He's fine. The operation was a success. He's coming in and out of consciousness."

He nodded at me then turned to Yusuf, who was awake but groggy. They spoke in Arabic. The new arrival asked him something. Yusuf mumbled a reply then turned his face away.

The man looked at me. "Who are you?" he asked.

"Geoff Manderson. I'm Yusuf's English tutor," I replied. "Who are you?"

"My name is Mustafa Farouk." He gave me a condescending stare. "I'm an advisor for the Libyan government. I monitor the progress of all the men in the program. Do you sit with all your students after their operations?"

"Not all. Just this one, in fact."

"Really? Why so special?"

Too late, I remembered Yusuf's injunction not to talk to his fellow Muslims. "I've been concerned for Yusuf's welfare, his state of mind."

"That's kind of you," he said. "Very unusual for a non-Muslim."

"Is it?"

I saw the man's eyes roam to my left hand.

"Not married?" he asked.

I was on the verge of telling him to mind his own business when Yusuf opened his eyes. He seemed to be taking in the two of us staring at one another in mutual dislike across his bed. Mustafa said something in Arabic. Yusuf made a short reply then Mustafa stood and left the room with a curt nod.

Yusuf's eyes rolled heavily towards me.

"Geef, what you tell Mustafa?"

"I said I am your tutor and that I care about your well-being."

He groaned. "I tell you don't say anything these people. Now he telling all Muslims."

"Telling them what? I *am* your tutor," I exclaimed. "Why does he care?"

An agonized look came over his features. "Is not good. Please don't talk."

I was suddenly fearful about whatever trouble I may have caused, the consequences of which were unknown to me.

I hadn't long to worry about it. At that moment, a clamoring came from the far end of the hallway. As it grew nearer, I looked up to see a surging crowd, a dozen men, some in wheelchairs and others on crutches, heading our way. For a moment, I felt alarm at this wild-looking bunch bearing down on us.

Ignoring me completely, they piled into the room, sitting or leaning against the walls wherever there was a space. Excited cries cut through the air when they saw that Yusuf was awake. His expression had changed from consternation to joy. Loud conversations in Arabic ensued. From time to time, one or another of the men would look briefly at me and nod. Clearly they were assessing me in some way, but what their impressions were I could not tell.

During a break in conversation, Yusuf's eyes turned to me, silently begging me not to do or say anything further that might give him away. I recalled his stories about how gays and lesbians back home were taken out to the desert and buried alive. I stood and nodded, giving a small wave as I slipped quietly from the room, resigned not to cause him further distress.

It wasn't until the following day, after a long night of anxiety over whatever problems I might have caused him, that I finally heard from Yusuf again. He telephoned from the hospital. Mustafa, he informed me, was a government watchdog who oversaw the men participating in the rehab program. He was a spy of sorts, reporting back everything about their activities. His suspicions had been aroused by this non-Muslim fraternizing with one of his wards.

"I am telling him you are friend of father from company. He is saying, 'Yusuf, why do you lie to me?'"

"I'm sorry," I said, chagrined that I had been unable to keep even such a small promise. "I told him I am your English tutor and I'm concerned about you. That's all he needs to know about me."

"Yes, Geef, I telling him this now. I saying I make a mistake from medication."

"Will he leave you alone?" I was alarmed at the web of deceit Yusuf felt necessary to create for his own safety.

"He is going be fine, but please not talking to him again. He is also speaking with my family."

"And the others?" I blurted out, unable to restrain myself. "The group who came in later? They kept looking at me, but no one said anything."

Yusuf laughed lightly.

"Yes," he said. "They are curious for you, sure. They are telling me, 'Yusuf, you are lucky having nice friend like that.'"

I felt relieved to hear that at least something about my presence in the hospital had been positive and that not everything I did caused him worry.

"Then I am good for you after all," I said, hoping to hear some sort of reassurance from him.

"You are good for me for everything, my love." There was a pause then he said, "One day, I will marry Geef."

"You even got the future tense right," I told him. "But be careful, because I'm going to hold you to that promise."

CEMETERY

It was a week or more since I'd spoken with my mother. Our conversations of late had been slow and halting. Neither of us openly acknowledged the futility of speaking when we disagreed on almost everything, though I know we both felt the weight of it. I see now that, at least in part, my attitude was to blame. I've never fully understood the enigma of family, that supposed blood tie linking you to people with whom you have little in common despite a shared past, when all about you are signs that if this were a war some of them might qualify as the enemy. It is one of the cruelest tricks of fate imaginable.

Nevertheless, I picked up the phone and called. We stumbled awkwardly through a conversation, both of us trying unsuccessfully to find common ground until one of us mentioned my father.

"We need to visit his grave," she said.

I felt a stab of guilt. I realized later that her suggestion was borne of good intentions, as a way of bringing us together, though at the time I felt she was doing it to punish me for not calling. But, as I often remind myself, if we don't have the freedom to choose then we have nothing. So I accepted.

The day was cold and rainy, as befits a visit to a cemetery. Otherwise, you might be tempted to go shopping or head to the beach instead. It struck me, as we drove through the gates at St. James' Cemetery, that my father would have passed by those same gates for years on his way to and from work without ever stopping to think that one day he would end up there permanently. The same might be said of the date which will eventually mark our exit from this life. Every year we engage in activities on that same date without knowing that one year it will prove our last on earth.

We parked inside the gate and proceeded on foot. It took my mother a while to locate the grave. It was as though, once he was buried and unable to cause her further discomfort, my father's physical location had ceased to concern her. Not that I could slight her for it. I hadn't visited since he was interred.

At long last, we found it. We stood there in silence staring at the marker as though something might unexpectedly appear on it, a rolling headline or message from the other side: *Hello, loved ones. … Thank you for coming. … How are you feeling today?*

In a way, it's reassuring to think we could experience the sort of contact with the other side that purportedly happens on such visits. But, of course, nothing happened. Instead, blue jays flitted in the branches above us as clouds scudded by. The sky opened a little and sent a brisk shower down, drenching us both without warning. If anything had been a sign of my father's presence, some indication of his feelings for us, then it might have been in that moment as we stood shivering and brushing ourselves dry. But then my father hadn't spent much time with us while he was alive, so why would that change after his death?

For a moment I wondered whether he had ever really wanted

children; obviously it was far too late to ask. Pity, I thought, as it might have resolved a few issues between us. It might even have helped me understand him better. In a different life I, too, might have had kids. Somehow I always assumed they would come along, but I like to think my relationship with them would have been dramatically different from the arms-length relationship I've had with my parents. I always wondered why anyone would go to the bother of having children only to neglect them, treating them like baggage rather than treasured possessions.

I turned aside, my eyes taking in the borders of the cemetery. When I looked back, I saw my mother wipe away a tear, whether for herself or for my father was impossible to say. But then it is probably just my uncharitable nature to think such things, she would have said. Just as they were not the parents I would have wished for myself, so too I was never the child they wanted. What a disappointment I must have been. Uncharitable, argumentative, homosexual. A total disaster in their eyes.

I used to think that wanting children — that desire to see yourself reproduced in another human being — was pure egotism. Now I see it as something more. I recognize in it the urge to share a part of yourself with others who might grow up to be like you. Yusuf and I had talked about having children. While I could never have borne him a child, I would love to have raised one with him.

As my mother and I stood there looking at my father's gravestone, I was conscious of my surname and the family crest emblazoned beneath.

GEORGE MANDERSON
1944-2012
Meae menor originis

I remembered the English translation, having memorized it as a child when my mother taught it to me: *Mindful of my origin*. Perhaps I had never been truly mindful of it before that moment.

It wasn't until we were trudging back to the gates, side by side beneath the dripping boughs, that my mother mentioned Yusuf.

"Do you think you can civilize him?" she asked.

Rather than anger me, the question elicited a guffaw.

Before I could reply, I heard her sigh.

"That is probably not the most diplomatic way to ask the question. You will have to forgive my ignorance of how to say these things properly, but I think you know what I'm asking."

Her honesty did something to soften my attitude toward her. I could see she was trying to connect with me, however ineffectually. It reminded me of how my father used to quiz me on the meaning of words. Did I know what such and such a word meant? Could I explain it? Could I use it properly in a sentence? At the time, I'd thought it a peculiar line of questioning, one that substituted for asking questions about my life that might have elicited what to him would have been unwanted answers. It wasn't until after his death that I understood: it had been his attempt to connect with me, his son the English tutor.

Without thinking, I found myself recounting the story of Yusuf's treachery toward me in trying to find a wife to marry for citizenship. But what I found appalling, she found amusing.

"And what did you do about it?" she asked, hiding a smile.

"I tried to remain dignified about it," I said, though that was not strictly true.

"How terribly English you sound. You take after me in that regard," she said with a brisk laugh. "And did you serve tea while discussing it with him?"

For a moment, I felt incensed by her insensitivity then suddenly I saw things through her eyes and glimpsed the ridiculousness of it all.

"I guess I should have," I replied.

We passed on to other topics, somehow made less opprobrious after that moment of levity. The afternoon, lost for me till then, suddenly came into focus and our talk flowed freely, as though a moment of grace had been granted us both.

It was the last conversation I had face to face with her. At least we managed to find a moment of mirth, a commonality. Maybe I should have tried harder, though God knows it's too late now.

FATHER

It was nearly a month since Yusuf had packed that suitcase of gifts to send home to Benghazi with a returning fellow student. Knowing communication from his war-torn country could be sporadic, and recognizing that his friend would need time to adjust to life back home, he expressed no surprise when the weeks went by and he heard nothing of its fate. As he described it, it was not uncommon for luggage to end up pilfered or simply to disappear between one airport and another. Even after the dissolution of the kleptocracy, old traditions persisted.

And for my part, knowing how much he'd spent on those gifts as the result of our numerous shopping expeditions together, I declared it a precarious route for such a pricey cargo. Yusuf waved the thought away. There were no other practical ways to deliver it, he told me. Once, he ventured to say that perhaps his friend hadn't called because he didn't want to tell him something had happened to the bag, in which case it wouldn't matter whether he called to report on it or not. It would have to be written off. He had already started filling another suitcase to give to the next student returning home. Such, to him, were the seemingly bottomless wells of Western living.

One bright morning, however, the student messaged him

on Facebook to say he had arrived safely back in his hometown and was going to deliver the gifts to Yusuf's family in the next day or two.

The news seemed to galvanize Yusuf. In the meantime, he worked on improving his English while he recovered from his operation. The shopping trips and the manic spending continued unabated. He never knew who would be leaving next, allowing him yet another opportunity to shower his family with gifts. For weeks the goods bulged in his dresser drawers and overflowed the closet in his room. On seeing them, you might think he had some sort of black market operation going on. Then, suddenly, someone would announce a pending departure and the drawers and shelves would empty out, only to be refilled again after a few days.

I was allowed to accompany him on these shopping expeditions, but they were clearly Yusuf's trips. He was in charge, taking his time to go through racks of scarves and women's blouses, displays of perfumes and hand creams. With imperious gestures, he indicated what he wanted to buy and how much he was willing to spend. His words to the shop assistants struck me almost as royal decrees: *I pay; I take; I want.*

In those moments, he seemed both ridiculous and magnificent as he walked the aisles of the stores with a boyish swagger, his buttocks flip-flopping from side to side as I followed behind. I realize he was constantly buying things for his family as a way of not being forgotten. It was his worst nightmare. The dead are forgotten and left behind, while the wounded are trapped in a state of limbo, shipped off to foreign countries for medical treatments. It was up to them to remind

[180]

the ones back home that they are still alive and preparing to return and re-enter their lives: *Never forget me, Geef.* It was his greatest fear. *I will never forget you, Yusuf.*

Sure enough, two days after receiving the message on Facebook, Yusuf got an email from Yasmin saying how happy they were for the gifts he had sent. Such luxuries! Nylons, perfumes, face creams, and scarves for his mother, grandmother, and sister. Shoes and socks for his brother, toys for his nephew, and a handsome sweater for his father.

As it turned out, Yusuf's father was back from the oil fields. His job had been disrupted by rebel insurgents and the workers had all been sent home. The entire family demanded an audience with Yusuf on Skype to express their gratitude. As much as I tried to avoid it, my attendance was deemed mandatory.

"Why do you want me there?" I asked. "Won't it be better if I am not? Aren't you worried they will be suspicious about your new friend?"

"No, Geef. You need to see Mahmood. Mahmood is nephew, three years old. Is going to love Uncle Geef."

I smiled indulgently, but it had suddenly dawned on me that I, too, was a conquest, an acquisition for his family to admire, something else for him to show off.

The Skype application shimmered into view, revealing the curious faces of people seated in an ordinary living room. I was nervous. How would they accept me? How would they view me? The women had their head scarves on, even Yusuf's grandmother, who was bedridden. His brother, Omar, skulked in the background, barking an occasional command to his family rather than directly engaging Yusuf in conversation. His resentment of his older brother was loud and clear as Yusuf described the shopping trips, the restaurants, while showing pride in his ever-expanding command of English.

The car Yusuf had bought online and shipped over had arrived. His brother was happily driving it around the city, he learned. Yusuf yelled at him in Arabic, which he later translated as something like, "You better be good to my car." Omar snarled something in return, though according to Yusuf he neglected to thank him for the extravagant gift.

The attention was now focused on me. Yasmin politely and formally addressed me. Her English was fluent, if a trifle stiff, though her questions never infringed on the personal. There were no awkward queries about my family or my marital status. Instead, she joked with me, asking whether her brother was really studying or just wasting my time.

"He's a good student," I replied truthfully.

I was surprised when Yusuf's father appeared on-screen. His English was even better than his daughter's. His pronunciation was correct and his vocabulary impressive.

"We are going to celebrate when Yusuf comes home," he told me. "And we will give great thanks to this wonderful new friend of my son's, who has been so generous and helpful during his time away. He says it is because of you that his healing has progressed so quickly, knowing he has a friend to rely on in another country far from his own."

I smiled and thanked him for the compliment, not daring to express my true thoughts, that as far as I was concerned their son was never going back to Libya.

There was a tense moment when Yusuf's nephew held up the toy monkey Yusuf had sent him. He proudly displayed the gift, but when asked who gave it to him, he replied that it had come from Uncle Omar.

Yusuf's sister went to great lengths to explain to her son that the gift had come from his Uncle Yusuf, who he was now talking to on-screen. The boy was obstinate, shaking his head while playing with the monkey's arms and insisting that his Uncle Omar had given him the precious toy.

I could see the pain in Yusuf's face. He was torn, proud to send his family gifts yet feeling estranged from them the longer he stayed away. In that moment, I saw a man caught between two worlds — a gay Muslim who petted dogs and drank alcohol, yet who still observed Ramadan and read from the Quran daily. He enjoyed a life with me, his lover, in one world, but still wished to obey his parents in another world that would never fully accept him for what he was and all he had become.

Perhaps he already knew this about himself or maybe he was still unaware of the dichotomy that existed within him. It was as though he believed he could keep straddling the divide so long as his family remained in one world and I in another. Or maybe it was I who was blind to the truth.

One by one, his family disappeared from the screen until only Yusuf's father remained. Apparently he wanted something like a man-to-man talk with me. He had met many non-Muslim men in his time, he told me, having worked both in his own country and abroad, in Germany in particular, but none had taken to him quite as I had taken to Yusuf. He expressed his gratitude for my actions, which to him must have seemed incomprehensible.

I made the gesture of hand to heart, saying simply, "Yusuf is my friend. He is important to me."

I could have said far more, but kept my thoughts to myself.

The topic turned again. He was out of work at present, he said apologetically, as though a man who wasn't working might be a man of wayward purpose. The rebels had set fire to the oil fields and the government was letting them burn. It was throwing the economy into turmoil once again after it had just started to regain some sort of balance since Gaddafi's overthrow.

Thinking of my meager tutor's income, I worried for a moment that he was about to ask to borrow money from me. In fact, he had nothing like that in mind. He merely wanted to give me an impression of what life in Libya was like at present for him and his fellow citizens.

"I wish I could do something to help," I said, genuinely moved by his story.

"Tell others," he said. "No one knows what is happening here. I fear the country will be at war again soon."

The conversation went on for some time until Yusuf interrupted us.

"Papa," he bellowed from across the room, his patience wearing thin. "You cannot talk so much. Geef is busy man. Very important."

I protested. Reluctantly, the older man bade me goodbye with a wish that we might speak again soon. I suddenly realized that he had been seeking my approval, rather than judging whether I was a good friend for his son. It hadn't occurred to me till that moment how much hope for Yusuf's future the family placed on my shoulders. He and Yusuf spoke briefly then rang off.

To my great surprise, the next day Yusuf informed me that after our conversation his father had expressed his total acceptance of our relationship.

"What does that mean?" I asked. "Does he know we sleep together?"

Yusuf shrugged shyly.

"My father, he say, 'Yusuf, need to enjoy your new life in Canada. Is very different from Libya.'"

Truer words, I thought.

"He say, Yusuf need to make Geef happy. Never did father have such nice non-Muslim friend like Geef in all his life."

"Maybe he should have slept with some of them," I said, to Yusuf's scandalized reaction.

ENGAGEMENT

It was another month before I spoke to Yusuf's parents again. A family call was convened. Yusuf's brother, Omar, had had an accident with the new car. It wasn't serious, but he didn't show up on Skype with the others that day, no doubt hoping to avoid his brother's ire.

Yusuf's father and I shared another moment on-screen. Once again, he thanked me for my friendship with his son. Yusuf had been telling them that his treatment was rounding up and he would be coming home soon. Although I had suspected as much, I was still surprised to hear him say this.

Yusuf and I had mostly avoided the thorny subject of citizenship since the operation. I had sincerely wanted him to heal, and had done my part by not putting obstacles in his path. By now I knew him well enough to realize that much of what he said was for show and, given time to reflect, he often changed his mind about things. I was also hoping that if I left it alone he might eventually come around to my way of thinking and reconsider the possibility of marrying me.

Yusuf and his father had another exchange in Arabic then the older man reverted to English when he spoke to me.

"It is good news for Yusuf," his father told me. "Maybe this fighting will stop and you can travel to Libya for his wedding."

For a moment, it didn't register. Then, suddenly, I felt as if I'd been punched in the head. I said nothing, merely nodded as though I were in agreement. At last, Yusuf said goodnight to his father. He closed his laptop and turned to me. My face must have told him everything I was feeling.

"Geef, I going get married." He watched me pensively as he spoke. "Father has arranged marriage to girl."

"What girl?"

"Girl in Libya."

"Your father has arranged a marriage to someone you don't even know?" I shook my head. "Is this true?"

"No, forget. Delete," he said with a frown.

At that moment, I no longer found his computer analogies with life all that amusing. "No delete!" I shouted. "What aren't you telling me?"

Slowly and quietly he explained that his parents had arranged for him to marry a young woman from a family in a village half an hour outside of Benghazi.

"And you accepted this?" I asked, aghast.

"Geef, I must."

It was like looking into the eye of a storm. The pure, clear light outlining the horizon moments before had suddenly vanished, taking with it the prospects of my continued life with Yusuf, leaving the sky in tattered ribbons as I stared into the future with a leaden gaze.

Jerod once described what it was like acting a role onstage, to get so worked up by his feelings that they could tear him apart while he was in character, only to come backstage after the show and sit before a mirror to remove the makeup and find a way back to his own life, his own existence, separate from all the emotions he'd just been living. I felt like that now. I was suddenly stripped of all my hopes and dreams the moment Yusuf uttered those words, revealing that I had been alone in believing them.

We'd had plans to go to a friend's place for dinner that evening, but I was in no mood for pretending. I was in no frame of mind to have Yusuf tell this friend of his impending engagement. Now that I'd introduced him to my neighbors, everyone had begun to ask about him. They were constantly suggesting future dinner engagements, extending well-meant invitations for get-togethers. Now I would have to start making excuses about his poor English or his unavailability due to medical reasons. I wasn't going to say I'd been thrown over for a woman he'd never even met, although that was the truth.

"Is this really what you want?" I asked him.

"It is, Geef."

So be it, I told myself.

Love and anger tore through me, each striving to annihilate the other. I was choking on rage, burning with shame at having been so oblivious as not to see what had been going on right under my nose. All I could think was that I needed to separate myself from him as far as possible. I would no longer call him my partner. From this moment, we would revert to being tutor and pupil.

"Geef," he said, placing his hand over his heart. "You are best for me. I am sorry."

"Me, too," I told him. "Because when you go home to get married, I will be left with nothing."

I put on my coat and went to the door.

"In fact," I said, "I think it's probably best if we end things right here."

He said nothing as I opened the door, waited, then left.

On my way back, I stopped off at a park. It was late. There was no one about except for the usual shades and half-shadows. I had sex with a handsome red-head, the only other person about who seemed more interested in sex than drugs. I did not enjoy it in the least. Afterwards, he offered to give me his number. I walked away from him without a word.

The next day, I ignored Yusuf's calls and cancelled our one-on-one classes. I didn't want a repeat of his suicidal urges that might end with him in the psychiatric ward, however, so I simply texted back to say that I was busy.

RECKLESS

The inevitable happened. There were one too many empty nights, one too many pleading messages on my phone waiting for me when I came home to my empty apartment. *Geef, I wighting for you.* Against my will, I called back. Against my will, I went to see him at the hotel, thinking I would deliver a stunning rebuke of his callous behavior toward me and still be able to resist him. That's not what happened. At his touch, I melted. I didn't have the strength to turn down his pleading invitation to stay the night.

But there was no going back. I knew our reunion was temporary at best. All that remained now was for Yusuf to complete his training on his artificial hand. Until then, he would not return to Libya willingly. He had everything in his future pinned on having the use of both hands, whether to practice medicine or to drive an ambulance in the fields of war again. The prosthetic was nearly ready and he was set to begin his first trials that month. Nevertheless, I felt I had been given that time to work on him, to get him to see reason, or at least what I thought of as reason.

It was no use. No matter what I did, it felt like I was fighting a losing battle. For every reason I came up with to make him reconsider his decision and stay, he had two reasons why he needed to return home to Benghazi, the most pressing being his upcoming nuptials.

I seldom spoke with my mother, and I had begun seeing less of David, effectively isolating myself from everyone who knew me. It was as if I'd thrown away a previous existence, feeble as it was, and created a new one bounded by Yusuf's needs. Having been willingly absorbed in his life up till then, I was now giving up my own.

I didn't understand the concept of duty toward family that he felt. Nevertheless, I looked on him as my family. Otherwise, I could not explain the devotion — the unswerving loyalty — I felt for him. In some intangible way, I was bound to him. It was an irresistible impulse I could neither avoid nor resist.

It was around this time that I heard from Jerod. His theatre contract was ending and he would soon be returning home. I needed to find another place to live. My sojourn, my idyll in the land of make-believe, was over.

When I looked at Yusuf in those days, it felt as though something inside me was dying. For a time, every part of him had filled me with wonder, giving me life and breath. Now he only took it away.

I thought of Baudelaire's famous disordering of the senses. Did I love this man because he was beautiful or did he appear beautiful because I loved him? If I had found him physically repellent, would I still have loved him as I did? I couldn't say.

As he lay stretched across the bed one evening when I stopped by after class, he asked me to massage his back. As usual, we'd been arguing over his decision to return to Libya.

Asking for a massage was his ploy to get me out of my foul mood, a ploy that usually ended up in a tangle of limbs and sex.

Today, however, I refused.

He glowered at me. "Geef, you are like a lazy wife."

"Oh, yes — I'm so lazy. 'Please, Geef, massage my back. Please Geef, make me a sandwich. Please Geef, do my homework. Please Geef, write a letter to my father.' Yes, yes, I'm very lazy. And while most men would rankle if you compared then to a woman, I on the other hand resent being called lazy, because I am absolutely *not* lazy."

He glared at me with suspicion for a moment before speaking. "What is 'rankle'?"

I shook my head. There was no escaping it. Behind the words, something in us had come undone. We both knew he was just biding his time.

Another day when I arrived at his hotel room, he staggered toward me with an odd grin pasted on his face. I smelled alcohol the moment he got close, as though he'd sprayed himself with it the way he did with cologne.

"What's going on?" I asked.

"Geef, I drunk," he stated blithely.

"I can see that. I meant why are you in this state?"

"I like alcohol."

"Yes, you like alcohol and petting dogs and having sex with men. You are a bad Muslim."

He laughed and reached out to hug me. He was trying to make nice. I was having none of it.

The story began to unfold. He'd been drinking in the hotel bar on the main floor. As usual, it had taken just two drinks to get him drunk. He had approached a woman, caressing her hair and telling her she was beautiful. Thinking he was about to assault her, she panicked and made a scene. Fortunately, Yusuf knew the security guard on duty. Knowing him to be otherwise well behaved, the guard had taken Yusuf aside and warned him not to cause trouble.

"'C'mon, Yusuf,' he tell me. You aren't that type.'"

"Did he mean not the type to cause trouble or not a heterosexual?" I asked, hoping to get a rise out of him.

He glared sullenly.

"You don't respect to Yusuf," he said calmly, reverting momentarily to his old, bad grammar.

"No, I don't respect you," I said. "Not when you're like this, drunk and acting stupid. What are you trying to do, get yourself thrown out of the hotel?"

Suddenly it dawned on me that that had probably been his intention, to be thrown out of both the hotel and the country. It was the only sure way to be rid of me and any rumors of his aberrant sexuality that might still be lingering after his association with me.

From that moment on I had no illusions left. I knew that when he left Canada, he fully intended to leave everything about us behind.

HANDS

The days were counting down. One afternoon Yusuf got word that his prosthetic hand had arrived. He called me excitedly to say he had seen it and was going to spend a week being trained on this bio-medical marvel that offered him a better future.

Ironically, I knew the firm that designed these prosthetic limbs had also created weaponized drones, funded by the money for defence research. The company that brought death and destruction to others was insuring its own longevity by creating technology to rebuild what it destroyed.

Despite this, I couldn't help being excited for him. His new hand would do everything his old hand had done save for one — it could not feel physical sensations like heat or cold or pain. It sounded perfect. I was tempted to ask if they might be able to make a prosthetic replacement for my heart once he was gone, something that would keep beating but feel nothing.

Never forget me, Geef. I will never forget you, Yusuf.

I was surprised when he called to invite me to sit in on the trials with him, but I did not turn him down. I wanted to be there for him.

The hand itself was a piece of bionic wonder, composed outwardly of black metal and plastic. I watched and listened as the technicians explained that with practice Yusuf would be able to use it to pick up something as thin as a dime.

"But how?" I blurted out. "It looks like a hand, but it simply straps on like a glove. What makes it work?"

The technician smiled. Evidently I was asking all the right questions.

"We are going to teach Yusuf to operate his new hand with neural impulses generated by his brain."

The lab workers were thorough and patient, taking him through the exercises step by step. I was amazed at Yusuf's diligence and seemingly inexhaustible patience as he listened and tried to repeat the things they asked him to do, over and over again, until he had mastered each one.

They videotaped his actions; by the end of the afternoon he had a thirty-minute program showing his progress. He was exhausted but elated when they unstrapped the hand and told him to sit back and take a breath.

They congratulated him, telling him he had far exceeded their expectations. He glowed with pleasure to hear this.

Yusuf and I left the laboratory together and went for coffee. He had come all this way with one goal in mind, and now he had obtained it. Never mind all the other distractions that I and so many others had put in his path along the way.

"You're a success," I told him. "Congratulations!"

"Yes," he agreed, smiling.

Underneath his newfound joy, however, I sensed a sadness as both of us avoided the subject of our inevitable separation. And, no matter what he professed, I also knew he was scared of what the future held. Perhaps he suspected, as I did, that a life for either of us without the other would not be worth living.

WINTER

Somehow, in our last few weeks together, I came to an acceptance of Yusuf's decision to return home. There was little to be gained now by trying to change his mind. I tried to look on it as a rational choice he was making rather than the conditioned response to his mother's haranguing and his father's hopes. In my eyes, Yusuf's fierce devotion to family ways and cultural traditions were things I didn't understand and never could accept.

The weather was changing, as was our language for one another. Nights were cool; a chill gripped the air as soon as the sun set. Yusuf no longer greeted me as warmly as he once had. No more the urgent kiss on my arrival or the leap into my arms that left me slightly off-balance before we fell headlong onto the bed in a joyous tangle of limbs. No more the urgent need to be intimate, either. Where once we had talked about moving in together when Yusuf finished his surgery, the topic was now clearly off the agenda. We were becoming little more than distant friends. Polite, cordial. At some point, without making an issue of it, I stopped sleeping over at the hotel. He did not complain.

My heart was broken but, wilfully disobedient comrade that it was, it would not accept my refusal to live, my ardent wish for it to stop beating in my chest when all I really longed for was a permanent end to the anguish it caused me.

One day Yusuf failed to show up for one of his final group lessons, which I had continued to teach after cancelling all private sessions with him. I called his room, but he didn't answer. I asked the other students, but no one knew if he had other plans. When the class was over, I dismissed the others and went upstairs. He opened the door with a smile on his face. I heard an unusual noise from within.

"Come, come," he said, ushering me inside. "I have a new friend."

I entered and looked around, but there was no one there. Then I heard a peeping sound and looked over to the window where a cage sat on a side table. Inside it was a beautiful bird with orange cheeks and black-and-white chest feathers.

"It is a zebra," he told me proudly.

At first I thought this was just one more of his zany jokes — a zebra in a cage — but in fact the bird was a zebra finch. It struck me as an odd thing to purchase if he was going away. For a moment, I looked on it as a sign of hope.

"Just to make the room fun," he said, glancing over his shoulder at the balcony. "Everything is grey outside now."

He was right. He was experiencing his first Canadian winter. The leaves had dropped off weeks before, but the first snows were yet to fly. Winter was approaching in stealth mode, but all the more earnestly for that.

We sat and talked, calmly and thoughtfully. He told me a little of the plans his family had been making for his marriage then, realizing he was hurting me, he changed the subject. It was unusually sensitive for him.

I told him that Jerod would soon be returning and that I had been looking for a new apartment. So far, I said, I had had no luck in finding anything.

"Geef, we are both changing, both moving," he said with a smile, as though this new commonality might yet bind us in unexpected ways.

"Yes, I said. It's true."

His smile faded as he realized what he had said. As I got up to leave, I saw him look at the cage wistfully.

"When I return home, I will be like a bird in a cage," he said in a barely audible whisper.

I didn't hear from him the following week. One afternoon, on impulse, I went up to his room after a session. I no longer had my door pass, so I knocked and waited till he called out for me to come in. The door was unlocked. I entered to find him staring out the balcony door. It was open and a cold wind blew into the room. That afternoon, the first snow had fallen and blanketed the courtyard below.

"Geef," he said sadly. "The bird has gone."

"What happened?"

"I forgot to close the cage. When the maid came to clean the room, the bird flew away." His eyes mournfully followed the path the bird had taken.

For a moment, I was more startled by his perfect English than by the news of the bird's escape.

"It will die," I said without thinking, rushing out onto the balcony in a forlorn effort to see if it had hovered nearby and might be coaxed back inside. There was no sign of it.

"I am going to die," he whispered.

"Don't be ridiculous," I said, angered that he would say such a thing. "It's just a bird."

LEAVING/HOME

I didn't want a protracted goodbye. As far as I was concerned, he was abandoning me. For all intents and purposes, our relationship was over. Once he chose the date I began closing off my heart to him, not answering his calls, not accepting his invitations to come over to chat, knowing full well where it could lead.

I told Marcus I wanted to pare down my tutoring schedule. I no longer had any reason to see Yusuf. And so I simply chose not to. For his part, he accepted my about-face and did not complain when I said I could no longer spend time with him. I think he respected me enough to realize I was not doing this to punish him, but rather to protect myself. Still, I did not cut him off entirely. I lacked the willpower for that. He was in my blood, in my heart, in my mind. He had been my family, my best friend, and my love.

Surprisingly, I found myself looking forward to the day he would leave, wanting to get past the torment, the inevitable consequences of when he left for good. As the day of his repatriation approached, however, he stepped up the late-night phone calls to me, calls I seldom returned.

Both he and my mother had reason to complain of my negligence in that regard. Once in a while I answered when

I saw his number on the call display. He never complained about my ignoring him, though I'm sure he knew I was doing it intentionally.

When we spoke on the few occasions I answered his calls, he was subdued and apologetic. I sensed that he was regretting his choice. Ironically, it was I who bolstered his decision, trying to make him feel better about the future he had chosen for himself. A future without an "us."

"You are going to have a beautiful family," I told him. "This is your duty now. One day you will tell your son how you helped liberate your country for his generation and all the generations to come."

And then one day he was gone. It was as simple as that. I did not offer to go to the airport with him; nor did he ask. I just looked up at the sky at the end of that day and knew he was no longer in the country.

Days went by, then weeks. The worst thing for me in all that time without him, after he had returned to Libya, was waking in the night. I, who had never really learned to be comfortable with another man in my bed, found I could no longer sleep alone.

Rather than lie there, thinking and regretting, I wandered the streets in a daze of confused feelings and abstract emotions. Still, there was no escape. No matter where I went, the city felt empty and lonely.

I never heard from him again after his return to Benghazi. Nor did I write.

Weeks went by. Most days I felt as if I were leaking emotion. I needed to love someone, I realized by then. But why did it have to be him? Maybe it was simply because he'd been there when the need came over me. Maybe that's all there was to it, the way the confluence of two cars moving in cross directions at the same time and place produces an accident.

I'd always assumed I would end up alone. Even as a child, I recall looking off to distant horizons and feeling the urge to vanish, to disappear from all that was familiar. It wasn't rational, but I felt it nonetheless. When I thought about the future, it always felt empty, as though there was nothing there at all. I can't explain this either.

One day a month after he left, I got an email message from his account. I opened it eagerly, but it wasn't from Yusuf. It was from his sister, Yasmin.

My dear lovely Geoff, she wrote in the same flowery terms Yusuf once used for me. *You may be surprise to hear from me, but Yusuf say he is always trusting you and if anything happen to him I must let you know. Today I write with the fearful news that my brother is missing for two days.*

My heart skipped a beat on reading those words. I dreaded what was to come, though I suspected I already knew the worst of what followed.

Yusuf meet this girl for his engagement then say, 'I do not love her. I cannot marry her,' causing great concern for both familys.

I think maybe he will contact his great friend Geoff to tell him what is happening. Please, if you hear from him? Let him know he must come home. We are very worried for this.

Yusuf say you are his best friend in whole world. I know you are a good man. If you can to help us, please do make him return.

I remain yours most sincerely,

Yasmin

I was as dumfounded to hear from her as I was to hear the sudden turn that Yusuf's story had taken. With a dawning sense of recognition, I realized my whole life had been leading to this moment. Somehow, without stopping to consider, I knew what I had to do. If this was a ploy on his part to get me over there, then it was working. On the other hand, if something had happened to him then I needed to be there to help. Barely taking time to think, I emailed Yasmin back and booked a flight for the next day.

In my haste, I didn't speak to my mother directly. Instead, I left her a voice message saying I was leaving town and hoped she would understand.

My last communication with David consisted of two brief sentences left on our respective answering machines. Perhaps by this point I'm sure we both realized the futility of speaking in person.

Mine: *I am going to Libya to find Yusuf and bring him back.*

His: *Now, finally, this is madness!*

BENGHAZI

Yusuf's hometown was not at all what I had expected, though I can hardly say what I expected. My first impressions were of a city trapped between a modern world that was in direct conflict with the old one it was trying to leave behind. The cars and many of the buildings looked contemporary. On the streets and in public squares, kids in T-shirts and jeans zipped by on skateboards, drinking Coca-Cola and plugged into iPods. Meanwhile, from the minarets, muezzins sent out shivering calls to prayer while men who looked as though they had been air-lifted straight from a Biblical costume drama scurried to respond.

Scars from the civil war were everywhere. Turn a corner and you found the ruins of a building that had been bombed or the hulking remains of burned-out vehicles pulled over to the side of the road sitting next to pristine high-rises surrounded by lofty palm trees. The air burned night and day with a feverish temperature. Dust gripped the roadways from one end of the city to another except where they bordered on the water.

Yusuf's father met me at the airport, his face long and haggard. He greeted me like a long-lost friend before launching into the tale of Yusuf's disappearance.

Slowly, reluctantly, he told me of Yusuf's betrayal at

the hands of his brother, Omar. Not long after he returned to Benghazi, Yusuf had met his bride-to-be. Immediately afterwards, he disappeared for a week. No one knew where he had gone. Then he showed up again, saying he could not accept the bride who had been chosen for him. His heart was not his own, he told them. He had left it behind in Canada.

The family did not understand. They assumed he meant there was another woman. But I understood all too well. Yusuf had come home clutching to the vain hope that he might forget me and fall in love all over again with a woman he did not even know. That was impossible. He had changed too much to go back to being what he was before he met me.

His family had tried to accept his decision. Yusuf was the eldest son, and his wishes must be honored, but there was still the matter of saving face with the girl's family. It was a grave insult for Yusuf to have turned her down after both families had agreed to the union.

It was his brother who had the hardest time accepting Yusuf's decision, his father said. When Yusuf announced that he was rejecting his bride-to-be, the two brothers stayed up all night arguing. In the end, Omar had turned against his brother. He had been in touch with a man named Moustafa Farouk, a man who had overseen Yusuf and the others back in Toronto. What Omar learned from Moustafa was not clear, but it had upset him greatly.

I felt trepidation on hearing the name. I pictured the arrogant, self-important young man I had run into in the hospital after Yusuf's operation, recalling how he had asked my marital status on noticing the absence of a wedding ring on my hand.

I knew Moustafa, I told Yusuf's father. Not well, but enough to know he was no friend of Yusuf's. Clearly it was he who had turned Omar against Yusuf, the scorpion waiting in the olive garden. I had crushed it in Yusuf's dreams, but not in real life.

The story continued as we drove through the city at twilight. Yusuf had tried to invoke his rightful place as elder brother, but from that moment on Omar would not respect him.

The pair went out together one night at Omar's invitation, supposedly to discuss the situation man-to-man. Omar had returned home at three in the morning with blood on his clothes. Despite the family's entreaties, he would not admit that anything had happened to his brother, saying only that Yusuf had gone off alone after their talk and that Omar had not seen him again.

Yusuf's mother cried on my arrival at the family home. Despite her worries she had gone all out, cooking a huge dinner for me. She entreated me to stay with them, but I declined, choosing to stay instead at a hotel a few blocks from the city center. So far, I had let them believe I had come to Libya on a business trip and that Yusuf's disappearance was entirely coincidental. I said that my company would be paying for the hotel.

Only Yusuf's sister knew why I was there.

Yasmine and I took to one another at once, perhaps because she was the most modernized of them all, or perhaps simply because I had answered her call to rescue her brother. She proudly introduced me to her son, Yusuf's cherished nephew, Mahmood. On meeting me, the boy showed me the toy monkey I had helped Yusuf buy what seemed like a lifetime ago.

In the center of the dinner table, in a room as contemporary-looking as any you might find in suburban North America, sat a framed picture of a smiling Yusuf. Seeing him there, I thought I heard him laugh and say something like, "Geef, why are you so slow to come?"

We sat down to eat. His mother had made lamb soup, delicately flavored and spicy. I recognized it as one of the dishes Yusuf had cooked for me. I bowed my head in prayer along with the others as they prepared to share their meal with me, the hoped-for savior of their son.

We were a small, sad bunch at the table, just Yusuf's mother and father and sister and me. The boy had already gone to bed. Omar was banished from the home. As far as they were concerned, he was no longer part of the family. Westerners, too, have their family squabbles, but for an Arab family to turn away a son is an act almost beyond imagining.

After dinner, I was shown to a small room, simply furnished. It was Yusuf's. I nearly wept when I saw his bionic hand sitting in its box on a shelf. This was one of the reasons the family did not believe Omar when he denied knowing where his brother was. Yusuf would never have left it behind willingly, his father said. Each day he practiced using it. Each day he was proud of his accomplishments.

Yusuf's father drove me to my hotel. I slept badly that night and each night thereafter. The morning calls to prayer alarmed me, serving to remind me that I was in a land that abhorred my very being.

Each day for four days I went out into the streets, armed

only with a photograph of Yusuf, but no one I spoke to had seen him. Each night I shared a meal with the family, who waited anxiously for news of Yusuf's return, though I brought none. They were insistent that I eat with them. For my part in the devil's bargain, I felt it was the least I could do.

One evening, after everyone else had retired, Yasmin stayed up to talk with me. She took off her head scarf. I looked at her.

"You are family," she said. "You are closer to Yusuf than anyone."

I nodded my acceptance of her explanation.

"I remember when first I see you," she said. "Yusuf is always chatting with me on the computer. I remember I call him on Skype one evening, but I can't see his face. 'Turn on your camera,' I tell him, but he will not. But later, after you are sleeping, he turn the camera on. He take the computer to where you are sleeping. 'This my boyfriend,' he said. 'This my true love.' He show how you are lying in bed with him, telling me how beautiful you are and how you are the best person he ever met. He is so proud of you!"

Tears came to her eyes and she stopped speaking.

"I will find Yusuf and bring him home," I promised.

News came the following day. Yasmin called me at the hotel. Her voice trembled as she related how she had heard from a family friend, a hospital worker from Yusuf's student days, who informed her that her brother was dead. Mustafa Farouk had told Omar about his relationship with me. In turn, Omar had betrayed Yusuf, selling him into the hands of men who took him out of town and stoned him to death.

I thought of Mustafa's cold, glittering eyes, his suspicious inquiries into whether or not I was married. Then I thought of Yusuf's brother, and how he had hated Yusuf's association with all things Western.

The men who killed Yusuf had denied him burial, Yasmin continued quietly. This was a grave desecration in Islamic tradition. I remembered Yusuf's grief over the fate of his fellow Freedom Fighter, Achmed, whose family had not been allowed to bury him.

On hearing of this, the family friend had gone to great lengths to find Yusuf's body and ascertain that it was him, Yasmin said. She had pretended to be a beggar woman searching among the ruins, but was unable to bury him with the rebel soldiers surrounding the burned-out villa.

"Tell me where he is."

"He is at Gaddafi's palace," she said.

She described how to find the place and the approximate location of Yusuf's body.

"Please," she pleaded. "Find him and bury him. If you go at night, no one is watching. You can bury him and come back here. You will not be seen. Then, when your time comes to die, you will be together with Yusuf in Paradise."

I went out the same day armed with sunglasses and a camera, as though I were nothing more than a tourist. It took almost an hour to find him, despite Yasmin's careful description of the location. At last I spotted him wedged between two slabs of concrete that hid his body from the road. Birds had plucked out his eyes, leaving him staring vacantly up at the sky. There was bruising all over his extremities and he smelled rank. I thought of his obsession with Calvin Klein cologne. It would have been an offense to him; he had always been so meticulous about hygiene in life.

I wiped away the dried blood with my sleeves and straightened his clothes. I couldn't risk burying him at that moment, knowing it would attract attention, but I took note of the location.

What are you so worried about? I had blithely asked him when he balked at my suggestion to marry me. *Geef, I worried for my life.*

I stood looking down at him, thinking of all the moments of intimacy between us. All the love, sex, and joy. It had come to nothing. There was nothing I could take from this moment and carry away with me that would gladden my heart for the time we had spent together. His prophecy had come true: *Geef, one day you are going to kill me.*

He had always known.

I walked in silence around the burned-out grounds. It was a wasteland. For a while, I felt nothing at all. Then the numbness turned to a blazing grief. I left thinking that there was no place on earth where I would ever feel whole again. I was thirty-five years old and there was nothing I could look forward to now.

I thought of my friend David, the all-wise and all-knowing, dispensing his wisdom to oblivious humans who slumbered in their ignorance, advising them of their folly as they persisted in their amorous pursuits, the sole prohibition that he himself could never enter the Land of Love.

STONES

The Bedouin believe they can read a man's future in a pile of rocks. But what can they see of a man's past and the many paths he has taken to get where he is today? I know how this story is going to end, but I can barely fathom how it began: I went out to a bar one night, and tried and failed at not meeting a boy. Despite whatever I may have said or believed, I know now that character truly is destiny, and we all make choices. I see clearly that our fates were already aligned before we even met and, by the time our affair was over, that neither of us would be able to live without the other.

It sounds like a cliché. And I, who have spent my life avoiding clichés and the traps that everyone else falls into, fell head-first into this one.

I think of his touch. I remember his fingers on my face, tangled in my hair, our bodies crushed together in moments of a love at times so searing that it pierced our souls and bound us together forever.

Forever.

Yet when I count back I see it's been a mere six months since it began.

It's dawn. The sun is struggling to rise over the Libyan desert, this vast place of sun and sand that never cools for long.

The rocks will hide his body. I've weighted him so the birds can't get at him again. I buried him with his head to the east. I'm not even sure that it's a proper Muslim burial, but I've done what I could.

There's no going back. I am no longer alone. I can hear the murmuring voices out there. They have recognized me, the infidel in their midst. They see what I have done.

I won't pretend that I am a hero. Heroes don't give up on life, though sometimes life gives up on them.

I brush the sand from my hands and light a cigarette. The condemned are allowed a last cigarette. I recall Yusuf's text the night I refused to take his calls, right before he had himself committed to the hospital's psychiatric ward: *You are my best friend, Geef. I wighting for you. Don't let me down.*

I am here, Yusuf. I haven't let you down.

The light dances before my eyes like a path shining across the sand, leading away from here. It won't be long. Soon someone will cast the first stone. And that stone will be followed by countless others. It won't matter. I won't be here.

Just before I place the final rock on his burial mound, I reach out and touch his hair one last time.

"Yusuf!" I cry. "Yusuf!"

ACKNOWLEDGEMENTS

Thanks to the Canada Council for the Arts, which invests in the creative lives of Canadian artists, and to the members of the jury who honoured me with a Mid-Career Explorations Grant for this book. Thanks also to David Tronetti, Felice Picano, Louis Ceci, Dawn Rae Downton, David Hunenberg, and Geordie Johnson for their patience in lending a critical eye to different versions of the manuscript. Knowing the difficult nature of the subject matter, I have tried to be as sensitive as possible in the telling of this story—their perspectives helped me achieve some semblance of balance in the viewpoints. And, of course, thanks to Sven Davisson and Rebel Satori for bringing me into the publishing fold.

Although this book is a work of fiction, my story was enriched greatly by my acquaintance with real-life Freedom Fighters, in particular EEM, who shared their experiences with me, contributing to and expanding my understanding not only of the Libyan Civil War, but of all conflicts. I salute those struggling for a better life, while wishing only peace and well-being for all. It's a big world out there. There's a place for everyone.

ABOUT THE AUTHOR

Jeffrey Round is an award-winning author, filmmaker, songwriter, and photographer. His books include the Lambda Award-winning Dan Sharp series, the comic Bradford Fairfax series, and the acclaimed war novel *The Honey Locust*. He directed Agatha Christie's stage classic, *The Mousetrap*, for three of its twenty-seven record-breaking years at Toronto Truck Theatre. His plays, films, and music videos have won multiple international awards, including the Luis Buñuel Memorial Award.